The
Merry XXXmas
Book of Erotica

Also edited by Alison Tyler:

Best Bondage Erotica
Best Bondage Erotica 2
Heat Wave: Sizzling Sex Stories
Three-Way: Erotic Stories

The
Merry XXXmas
Book of Erotica

Edited by Alison Tyler

CLEIS
PRESS

Published in the United States by Cleis Press Inc., P.O. Box 14697, San Francisco, California 94114.

Printed in the United States.
Cover design: Scott Idleman
Cover photograph: Susan Egan
Text design: Frank Wiedemann
Cleis Press logo art: Juana Alicia
First Edition.
10 9 8 7 6 5 4 3 2 1

To SAM.

Acknowledgments

To those who make *all* my seasons merry: Violet Blue, Eliza Castle, Barbara Pizio, Thomas S. Roche, Kerri Sharp, Rachel Kramer Bussel, Michele Zipp, and Felice Newman and Frédérique Delacoste.

He's going to find out who's naughty and nice...

—"Santa Claus Is Coming to Town"

Contents

Introduction

It's beginning to look a lot like Christmas. How do I know? Not because of silvery frost on the rooftops or canned Christmas carols echoing endlessly through my head. I can tell because I'm feeling extra naughty…desperately naughty, sinfully naughty. Naughty enough to lick a fiery red and white peppermint stick and then slip it slowly down my body to the split between my thighs. Naughty enough to tie myself up with a glossy crimson satin ribbon and wait under the tree for that lucky someone to unwrap me. Naughty enough to get wet every single time I spy a department store Santa—which can make shopping for holiday gifts a downright X-rated experience.

This time of year, my mind is always filled to bursting with erotic visions. But I'm sure that Santa won't be bringing me a lump of coal as payback for my rather politically-incorrect holiday spirit. No, I have faith that my secret Santa has far sexier treats in store for me. Treats that come cleverly wrapped in plain brown paper. You see, Santa knows by now that I'm much more naughty than nice. For me, nice isn't an option. 'Cause nice girls are never caught kissing Santa—that's for sure.

The characters in this triple-X collection have found their way onto Santa's naughty list, as well. Lovers are "Rapt," in Saskia Walker's cab fantasy, before they are "Unwrapped," in Ayre Riley's girl-in-charge piece. The delightful Kat knows exactly what to ask a sexy female Santa for in Lynne Jamneck's "What I Really Want for Christmas" while the creative coed in erotic mastermind Thomas S. Roche's "Here Comes Santa Claus" blows all of her Christmas money in a sex toy store to make sure she gets what *she* really wants for Christmas. M. Christian turns the O. Henry classic "The Gift of the Magi" on its head in "When the Giving Got Good," while Michelle Houston investigates a bold new location for a sprig of mistletoe. Rachel Kramer Bussel's "Last-Minute Shopping" is a delicious seasonal fantasy come true, and "You Better Not Pout" by Dante Davidson brings an old holiday standard to life in a brand-new way. I challenge anyone to write a more twisted tale about holiday decorating than Alex Mendra's "Trimming the Tree." And nobody knows how to stuff a stocking better than Santa himself in Tsaurah Litzky's little bit of Christmas magic, "Gifts from Santa."

The twenty-one stories in this book are hot enough to melt the snow on anybody's rooftop. They're bound to replace visions of sugarplums with visions of sex toys, create lustful yearnings for anyone dressed in red felt and a fake white beard, and make the concept of elf sex sound like a really good idea. Most importantly, the stories here are destined to instill in you a lust for erotic adventure all year round.

And that's all *I* really want for Christmas.

Here's wishing a very merry XXXmas to you and all the naughty boys and girls on your list.

Alison Tyler

Gifts from Santa
Tsaurah Litzky

HO, HO, HO, it's Santa Claus. I'm dreaming he's sliding down my chimney with a big, red cock. When he comes to stand in front of my bed, I see how fine and strong that big red cock is and I want him to put it in the silky stocking I have between my legs.

When I tell him I want his cock in my stocking, he asks me a question: "Have you been a good girl?" I have to say no. I have not been a good girl at all. I confess I always eat the icing off the cake. I'll tell any fib to get a date. I play footsie with my friend Trina's husband, Wally, when I sit next to him at dinner parties. I steal lingerie from department stores. I goose strange men and women when I find myself pressed against them during rush hour on the subway. They look around but never realize it's me.

"You *have* been a very bad girl indeed," Santa tells me. "You need a thorough spanking before Santa can will fill your stocking." He tells me to throw off the covers.

I obey Santa. I am not wearing anything except my panties. Santa looks me up and down. "You are prettier than plum pudding," he says. Then Santa tells me to slip off my panties, the new white silk ones with cute pink pussycats printed on them. I stole them from Saks Fifth Avenue just last week by stuffing them inside my jeans pocket as if they were a hanky. When I slip them off, Santa takes the purloined panties from me and sniffs the crotch.

"You certainly have been a naughty, naughty girl," he says, and then he sniffs my panties some more. His red cock grows even bigger. It changes shape as it swells and now it looks like a spatula or a giant red paddle.

Santa tells me to get on all fours. "Now lift up your honey-bunny bun, higher," Santa says. "That's right," says Santa. "Now you are acting like a good girl should." He chuckles approvingly, "Ho, ho, ho."

He begins to spank me with his paddle-cock. He smacks my ass again and deliciously again with his sturdy tool. At first he spanks with a loving touch, lightly, three gentle little taps on my right asscheek, three on the left, then four on each side, then five. Soon, Santa starts to spank me harder, *smack, smack, smack!* I never imagined Santa would have a thing for spanking, but he really gets into it. He's an expert. He knows when to take his time and he knows when to speed up. I wonder if he spanks the elves for practice; is that how he gets them to behave? I want to ask him but I don't want to interrupt his concentration as he steadily, rhythmically paddles me. He uses the strength of his whole arm to bring his paddle-cock down, now smacking me super vigorously.

"Stop, stop, no, no, no!" I squeal. My whole ass is stinging, tingling, but I like it; oh, how I like it. The more it stings, the more I like it. I look back and see my butt has taken on a deep, bright red strawberry color almost the same shade as Santa's thick, scarlet cock.

"Enough, enough, Santa, please stop," I cry, but I don't mean it. It feels like my ass is on fire, but the fire is not burning me, just making the love juices inside me simmer to a fine boil. I relax and let the delicious heat wash through my cunny; it spreads up to my tits and down to my toes. Now I am purring like a kitten being stroked. Maybe Santa liked it better when I was squealing "Stop" and "No" because he suddenly ceases spanking me. He must know how much I want more by the way I keep purring and pushing my throbbing bum up to him in invitation, shaking it.

Maybe Santa wants to show me who is boss, or maybe Santa is just a tease. "That's enough," he says. "You can roll over on your back now." Gingerly, I flip over. The sheets feel soothing and cool against my tender rump.

I look up at Santa. His eyes are twinkling, and his face is very rosy, as if he had just been shoveling snow. His cock is pointing right at me. It doesn't look like a paddle anymore but it is still very big, the size of a generous salami. "I hope you've learned your lesson, and next year you'll try to behave," he says. "No way," I tell him with a grin and he winks at me. "Ho, ho, ho," he bellows. "You are a very smart girl indeed."

"Oh Santa, thank you," I say. I tell him that this has been the very best spanking I've ever had.

"I have something else very special for a smart, sassy girl like you," he says.

He lowers his head and attaches his big, pink Santa mouth to one of my teeny nipples. He starts to suck it slowly, savoring it, licking it, flicking his fat tongue back and forth. This makes me feel very, very nice and my silky stocking gets all wet and sticky. Santa's long, stiff white whiskers are tickling my tummy as he sucks and I start to giggle. Santa lifts his lips off my nipple.

"I like a jolly, merry girl, particularly one who can learn from a good spanking," he says. "Now Santa is going to give you something to really laugh about. Soon, you will be roaring with glee."

Santa puts his chubby hand between my legs and sticks a finger right into my slit. I'm all juicy and slippery, and his darting digit feels so nice dancing up inside me. He moves it in and out, out and in. When he pulls it all the way out, it is covered with the sticky syrup from between my legs. Santa puts the sticky finger in his mouth. He sucks it for a while, then says, "Dee-licious. This tastes better than a peppermint candy cane. Now Santa has a great big candy cane for you. Have a taste."

He puts his hands out and spreads my legs, kneels over me, and guides his cock into the sticky place between them. It feels so sweet, moving in and out of me; the deeper the sweeter. My insides begin to melt with pleasure, but then there is an inter-ruption—an abrupt pounding on the ceiling above, a stamp, stamp, stamping sound.

Santa pauses and looks up, half inside me, half out. "It's my reindeer," he says. "Be patient," he calls up, his voice ringing out like a chime. "Be patient, Dasher and Dancer, Donner and Blitzen, Santa's coming. I'm coming, I'm coming...."

From above we hear a few faint neighs and the sound of the sleigh bells. Santa starts to move in and out of me again, faster and faster. The sweet feeling between my legs gets more intense and I start to come.

Suddenly Santa bursts into song: "Jingle bells, jingle bells, jingle all the way! Oh, what fun it is to ride in a one-horse open sleigh." His mellifluous voice rises to a crescendo as he plunges even deeper inside me and he comes too. I fell very, very happy. Santa is happy too; he falls down on top of me and gives me a big hug. "Merry, merry Christmas," he whispers in my ear. "Did you like your gift?"

"Oh, yes, yes, Santa," I say. I can feel Santa's hot jism running down the inside of my leg. It smells like a toasted marshmallow. I want to show Santa just how much I like it by asking him to rub it all over me, but then we hear the bells jingling above us again. Santa stands up and tucks his versatile thing back inside his trousers.

"I have one more gift for you," he says. He reaches into his pocket and pulls out a tiny red wooden paddle on a green velvet ribbon. It is adorable, just like Santa. He hangs it around my neck. I tell him that I love it and will wear it every day.

"I have to go now," Santa says. "I have lots of other sweet girls to visit tonight. But remember, if you behave"—he winks at me again—"it's a candy cane world." I understand just what Santa means. "I hope you're right, Santa," I say.

"Be a spanking good girl like Santa taught you and you can count on it," he replies. Santa pats me tenderly on the head, and with a final, "Ho, ho, ho," he turns and vanishes back up the chimney.

Spider Monkey Loves Rudolph
Tom Piccirilli

Sometimes the low point of your life doesn't come when you're lying in the gutter smelling like the bottom of a bottle of scotch, or when your wife finally leaves you, or when you crap out for the last time at a casino and realize you've gambled away your kid's college fund.

Mine was being at this Christmas party in Beverly Hills, thrown by a rich producer much younger than me, attended by beautiful high-powered movers much younger than me, and whose guest of honor was a screenwriter much younger and much more successful than me.

I was caught vacillating between drowning my hideous failure self in the pool, which was the size of a lake, or the hot tub, which was the size of an Olympic pool.

I'd spent most of my career writing scripts about Zypho, an alien being from "beyond the edge of space" that used its tentacles to suck out either brain or vaginal juices depending on what market we were attempting to hit. I'd seen Zypho lopped down to a G-rated kiddie show in Japan, and it was also a hit on the adult market thanks to a few clumsily inserted scenes. With a handheld camera Monty had managed to tune the flick up to triple-X stature that appealed to the kink crowd. Tentacles or rubber dildos, nobody really gave a shit so long as they went in the right slot.

The only reason I was there was because my agent and sometime producer Monty Stobbs thought it would be good for us to rub elbows with the Hollywood elite. He said the rich producer owed him one from some minor hit they'd worked on together years before, but it wasn't until we arrived that I realized I'd crashed the party. Luckily, it would be too gauche and provincial for them to throw me out on Christmas Eve.

So far, the only elbow-rubbing I was doing was when I had to push my way through the crowd while the wealthy kids stared at me in confusion, wondering how someone with a streak of gray in his hair wasn't using a walker.

I orbited various groups of celebrity actors and musicians, keying in on vacuous conversations punctuated with well-practiced titters and giggles and hyped by hard liquor. Some of them were dressed up like elves or wearing Santa costumes. They were organizing a wet T-shirt contest out by the pool that looked like a lake, so I had to forestall my plans for drowning myself there. I turned to the hot tub and there were twelve people up to their necks in the bubbling waters. They were trying to stare lustfully at one another except they were thrown off by a spider monkey hanging from the towel rack.

If I had my druthers, I wouldn't want to screw anybody in sight of a spider monkey either. But then again, I was thirty-eight years old and I'd never had my druthers. I wasn't overly certain what a druther was, but the lack of it somehow added to my funk.

At around midnight the sexual tension of the party was beginning to reach critical mass. Twice I'd been asked if I had any coke and twice I'd been asked to bring the lady a wine spritzer. I had been feeling underdressed, which was ironic now that people were beginning to disrobe, and those who weren't wore elf outfits. I hadn't seen Monty for over an hour.

Despite my fear that there might be more animals indigenous to the South American rain forests stalking about the place, I started trying doors looking for a way out. I thought I would crack Monty in the mouth and then thumb a ride home to my squalid pad in East Hollywood.

Finally, I opened a door and there he was.

"Holy Christ!" I shouted.

"Help me!" Monty screamed.

It took me about a minute to comprehend the entirety of the scene before me, and then another five or so for me to stop guffawing so hard that I felt my pancreas shaking loose.

Someone with a serious mad on had done ole Monty wrong. He was handcuffed wrist and ankle to the four-poster bed. He'd been dressed up like Rudolph, replete with a red rubber ball nose and reindeer antlers with a tightened chin strap to hold them in place on his head. There were trailing reins tied down over his chest and a collar with big jingly bells on it. He even had booties on that looked like hooves.

"Stop laughing, damn it," he whined.

"I've got to admit, Monty," I told him, "I was feeling a little low tonight, but you've perked me right up."

"Get me out of here!"

"What the hell happened?"

"You remember the girl I was with?"

"No."

"Well, apparently she's a screenwriter, sent me something once and I rejected it."

"You've never rejected anything in your career, Monty. What's the real story?"

"I guess I met with her and tried to make her a year or two ago. She says I groped her and she threw wine in my face."

"And you don't remember?"

"You know how many women have thrown wine in my face?"

"Sorry, I forgot who I was talking to for a second. Jesus Christ, Monty, she even brought four sets of handcuffs. And these booties! You must've *really* pissed that lady off."

"All you fucking writers are too sensitive. Get me loose, will ya?"

The four-poster was a massive metal job with welded joints. The headboard was as solid as the grille on a '57 Chevy. "No way, Monty."

"Goddammit! You've got to go get a hacksaw."

"Where am I going to get a hacksaw in Beverly Hills on Christmas Eve?"

"You're right. You've got to go get the key from her. You've got to apologize for me."

"What's her name?"

"I don't know. I wasn't thinking long term."

Only Monty would think that asking a woman's name might be considered a long-term relationship. "What's she look like?"

"Raven hair, a nice rack."

"There's about four hundred ladies like that out there."

"I know, I know! Ah, well…she's got a sharp look about her. Thoughtful."

"That's the best you can do?"

"I wasn't in the mood to discuss Kierkegaard."

I started to shut the door and he screamed, "Wait! At least come take this shit off me!"

"No," I told him. "You're right, we writers are too sensitive. You're getting off easy. I was ready to break your jaw for dragging me to this party and grinding down what little ego I have left. Sit tight, and don't make too much noise. There's a spider monkey roaming around that might come and eat your eyes out."

I slammed the door before he could say anything more.

The party crowd had somehow doubled since midnight, and they were singing now. They had *It's a Wonderful Life* on a big-screen plasma TV. In another corner they were singing "Let It Snow." What I would've given to be walking around Rockefeller Center in Manhattan and watching the ice-skaters. For the last three days I'd been keeping my eye on the Weather Channel. It was supposed to snow in New York tonight. I'd never get used to Christmas in Hollywood.

The first two qualities were easy enough to check off so far as Monty's lady was concerned—raven hair and a nice rack. The thoughtful expression was a little more difficult to find. It took me a while.

She was standing off alone from the crowd and there was a tinge of sadness to her eyes. Monty would mistake that for thoughtfulness. Even if I hadn't already fallen in love with her for dressing Monty up like Rudolph, I thought, the melancholy gaze could well drive me over the big edge.

She was dressed in a demure red dress that made me think

of a sexy Mrs. Kringle. The black hair was cut into soft waves that framed her lovely heart-shaped face. She wasn't quite smiling, and yet she appeared to be amused by all that was going on around her. She seemed as if she felt about as out of place as I did.

I walked up and asked, "You wouldn't happen to have the key to four sets of handcuffs, would you?"

"That's got to be the worst opening line I've ever heard," she said.

"Under normal circumstances, I'd agree with you."

She sipped her cosmopolitan and gave me those eyes again. "Is that prick a friend of yours?"

"Agents don't have friends, only clients."

"Is he thinking of pressing charges?"

"It would be your word against his, which is why he's lost every court case he's ever been involved in. I doubt he'd want this one to go before a jury. Oh yeah, where'd you get those little booties?"

"At a sex shop on Rodeo Drive."

"Jesus Christ, people actually wear them during sex?"

"I don't understand it either."

"Did you bring them specifically for Monty?"

"Him or four or five other guys."

"You've really had it rough, haven't you?"

It brought the sorrow and anger out in full bloom. For a second she must've thought I was mocking her, but after she stared intently at me she realized I wasn't. "Are you in a rush to get back to him?"

"Hell no, I'm only now starting to get my vision back. It was quite a scene."

She was beginning to smile a little, and that started to do things deep inside my chest.

"You don't belong here either," she said.

"No. What's your name?"

"Katherine. What's yours?"

I told her and she immediately rattled off the titles to three ultra low-budget horror flicks I'd written for Monty. They'd all started out as serious explorations of the nature of relationships in the modern world and somehow ended up full of big-titted scream queens being chased through haunted houses in their skivvies. She tried to find something nice to say about my work but couldn't quite do it. I gave her points for trying.

"Come on," she said. "I can't breathe in here."

She led me out to the yard, beyond the pool and then beyond a group of drunken revelers playing volleyball with a water-filled condom, and even beyond the minor-celebrity actress entwined with the minor-celebrity director who'd passed out on a chaise lounge about six seconds before actual coitus. If the spider monkey went after the director's peeled banana he was going to wake up mighty damn quick.

Katherine and I wandered the estate discussing writing and the vagaries of Los Angeles, and our general disappointments and occasional triumphs. At the end of our litanies we sort of fell into each other, at first just hugging very tightly before we worked toward a kiss.

It was soft and a little painful and altogether enchanting. The warm wind blew across our bodies, and when I kissed her again I felt a drop of sweat slide from her forehead and against my lips.

"I want you," she said.

"Even without the hoof booties or the little red nose?"

"Especially without those."

"Well, okay then."

It brought a soft throaty chuckle out of her that worked itself into me until I was hard and needy. We lay in the grass. She reached up to unfasten the buttons of my shirt, then pressed her palm to my chest and dug her fingernails in. She seemed a bit surprised that I was made of flesh and not film stock. I could see that Monty hadn't been the only bastard she'd run into.

She undid my pants and yanked them off me. Then she drew her dress halfway up and no further. She didn't have on any panties. Apparently she expected me to just climb on. The animal urge was there, but I gently drew her dress up over her head and spent a while kissing her breasts. At first I could feel her resistance, as if her own desires embarrassed her, but after a few minutes of my massaging and licking her nipples I could sense her fear falling away. Again the throaty chuckle worked free from her and I pressed my erection forward into her hand.

Pumping softly but with real intent, she brought me to a full hard-on. She spit in her hand and jerked me faster as I jutted on my knees. She leaned up and kissed me passionately and pressed my cock across her belly.

I liked the feel of her skin. She lowered her mouth to my cock and I grabbed her hair and held her to me, easing in and fucking her throat.

She groaned deeply and again, and I realized she was saying my name with my cock in her mouth. It was a very strange assertion of my existence.

She began sucking and rubbing more forcefully until I grunted and eased her chin back further until my prick popped out. She lay aside and looked at me and broke into a grin. I let out a groan.

I held her legs open and kissed her knees and licked her

calves and then fitted myself at the edge of her cunt and waited. She laughed again and bucked forward and I was in her.

"Katherine," I said.

"Again," she told me.

"Katherine."

"Yes."

I filled her pussy tightly and her juices already flowed around me and dappled my pubic hair. I plunged into her and kept my pacing slow so she'd know I meant every thrust. We all need affirmation. Katherine moaned and the sweat streamed across her face. I got in close and licked her cheeks, kissed her nose, ran my lips against her eyes. The veins in her throat stood out and I nipped them with my teeth. She kept her eyes open and locked on mine. "Don't close your eyes," she said.

"I won't."

"Look at me," she groaned.

"I will."

My cock continued to heat up inside her as she quickened her pace, and I began to feel her orgasm growing. Her tits bounced to our rhythm and I locked my hands on her hips and pulled her up onto me. We were both covered in grass stains and breathing heavily as the wind blew hotter and hotter around us. My sweat splashed across her and she raised her hands to dig into my chest again. I liked the honest feel of her nails. She grunted and stiffened as I slammed even more deeply into her.

We kept our eyes open. She was on the edge and so was I. We stayed there for longer than seemed humanly possible. I leaned down until we were nose to nose, and said, "You're so beautiful, Katherine." Her pussy tightened so hard I let out a yelp. She let out a cry and so did I and my come filled her.

I dropped forward and drew her onto her side with me, but didn't slip free from her. We relaxed like that for a long time, gently stroking, the tips of our tongues toying with one another.

It took us a while to unwrap ourselves and get dressed again, and when we did we walked with our arms wrapped tightly around each other's waist as if trying to hold on to some lost hope that had been restored—perhaps only for the night, perhaps longer.

"We still need to go let Monty loose."

She didn't have a handbag and I could attest to the fact that she had no key on her. She caught my puzzled look and said, "They're trick cuffs. There's a tiny switch on them. You just have to press it."

"Cup your hand and pretend there's a key or he'll lose his mind."

When we got back to the house it took me three tries to find the right room.

I opened the door and saw the spider monkey was perched on Monty's head like Zypho trying to suck out brain juices, holding on to an antler in one hand and gripping a tuft of Monty's hair in the other. Monty had his eyes tightly scrunched shut in terror.

"Dude," I said, "you made a friend!"

"It's been on my head like it's sitting on an egg!"

Katherine pretended to use a key to open the four sets of cuffs. I leaned over and the monkey made a soft noise and jumped into my arms. Monty had lost feeling in his limbs and it took him a few minutes to get his circulation going again. He tentatively opened his eyes.

"Where's my clothes?" he asked.

"I threw them out the window," Katherine said.

"You…," he said. "You…!"

Katherine smiled at him. "Yes, me. But don't bother looking down there, I think somebody stole them."

"You…!"

"Don't be nasty, Monty," I said. "It's Christmas Day. The only reason Scrooge didn't die alone and unloved was because he learned his lesson."

"Oh, fuck you people!" He tore off the antlers and the plastic red nose, but the reins and the collar were heavy with buckles and straps and Monty didn't have enough feeling in his hands yet to work them.

It was almost four A.M. and the temperature had broken ninety. Rudolph pranced across the wide lawn and hopped into the back of his BMW. Katherine got in the passenger side and I got in and drove.

In New York they were probably inside their apartments waking up with their trees and their presents, staring out at a blizzard, promising their kids a morning sled race in the park. Katherine took my hand and started singing "Let It Snow," and I put the air conditioner on full blast until Monty was shivering so hard his collar jangled in tune with the song.

A Very Naughty Elf
Felix D'Angelo

Traveling during the holidays—it's a bitch. When I called from Phoenix to tell you there was another delay, that I wouldn't be home until two in the morning, I could positively *see* you pouting. "I'd hoped we could have a little Christmas fun," you told me.

"Tomorrow," I said. "Tomorrow's Christmas. We'll sleep in and open our presents whenever we feel like it."

"I was hoping you'd open your present tonight," you said with a rich sense of mischief in your voice. "I think you're going to like it."

"Tomorrow morning," I repeated.

My car is freezing cold after a week in long-term parking. The long bus ride out to the distant lot seems to take forever, and it's more like three when I finally pull into the driveway.

I shouldn't be surprised to see milk and cookies waiting for me in the living room, laid out on the little end table near the chimney. But I *am* surprised to see, suddenly, what you had in mind for "Christmas fun."

I suppose I should have figured it out when the package came from Costume Mart. "Is *that* my present?" I'd asked naughtily. "It's *a* present," you'd said. "But not for you."

"Who, then?"

You'd kissed me and said, "For someone very naughty." And then you'd smiled.

Now I know what it was you bought: a furry red Santa suit, complete with a big black belt and fuzzy white cap, beautifully displayed on the sofa. I eye the suit suspiciously as I take a cookie from the plate, then have a sip of milk rendered icy by December's chill. There's a note on the table, in your handwriting, in glittery red gel ink: *More treats in the bedroom, Santa.*

In case I hadn't already figured it out, now I know: you are the biggest pervert in the world.

I tiptoe down the hallway and find the bedroom door open. You've left the bedside lamp on, but you're quite asleep—illuminated in the soft light with a dirty paperback propped open, the spine broken, next to you on the bed. You're dressed exquisitely for the occasion. You're wearing green stockings, green high heels, and a sparkling green garter belt with a matching G-string, not to mention a green push-up bra. The elf cap, of course, is strictly dime-store fare, but it has slipped off your head and lies forgotten next to the dirty book. The metallic green lip gloss is surely from the dime store, too, and I have to admit that it does complete the costume nicely. "The Carol of the Bells" plays softly on the clock radio next to the bed.

I say your name, but you don't stir. I guess you couldn't wait for Santa to finish his rounds.

As exhausted as I am after almost twelve hours of traveling, I'm not going to let you miss out on your Christmas Eve fantasy. After all, it's the elves' night off, and Santa's got a present for your stocking, hardening quickly as I strip myself out of my jeans and underwear. I leave my clothes scattered across the living room and climb commando into the furry pants, feeling my hard cock rub on the soft fabric. I button the jacket over my sweater and sit down on the sofa to pull on the big knee-high black boots, shimmering PVC—you thought of everything, but I bet you didn't get *these* boots at Costume Mart.

I'm so distracted by the costume, in fact, that I don't immediately notice the shreds of red paper littered around the Christmas tree. The box I so carefully wrapped is torn open, and the present I bought you is gone. Before I put the boots on, I tiptoe back down the hall to peer into the bedroom again—and see you definitely didn't wait for Santa to finish his rounds. The surprise vibrator lies next to the bed, its cord snaking around to the power strip in the corner.

I return to the living room and don the boots. As I walk down the hall for the third time, I don't tiptoe; my boots make a heavy rhythmic pulse against the hardwood. Nearing the bedroom, I unbuckle the three-inch-wide leather belt and slip it out of the belt loops.

The clock radio is playing "Santa Claus Is Coming to Town," a maudlin version by some fourth-rate '60s pop singer. As if it wasn't naughty enough opening your present early, you've left the radio tuned to carols—Santa is positively sick of Christmas carols.

Your eyes pop open and you look at me, bewildered for

a moment. Then you smile. "Merry Christmas, Santa," you say before your eyes flicker down to the big thick belt in my hands and you see the stern look on my face.

"You've been a very naughty elf," I tell you.

A shiver goes through you—a familiar sight in late December, but it's not a shiver of cold; though the living room's freezing, the vents in the bedroom are open and the small, plushly furnished room is warm enough to cook a goose. I kick the door closed behind me to hold in the warmth and start toward the bed.

"Sorry, Santa," you say naughtily. "An elf gets horny waiting for her master to get back to the North Pole."

"I've got your North Pole right here," I tell you. Sitting down on the side of the bed I stroke your mop of blonde hair, then pull you over my knee. As I do, the light from the bedside lamp flickers across your hair and I see you've even dyed the tips green. That makes me pull harder and wrestle you into position with greater urgency. You yelp, but don't resist; on the contrary, you slide smoothly into proper position, stretched across my lap with your ass in the air, the tiny strap of your sparkly silver G-string the only thing covering your perfect ass.

"Naughty elf," I say, and bring the belt down across your upper thighs. You whimper and squirm, but obediently push your elf ass up toward me. I strap you harder, and the shudder through your body is stronger this time. You wriggle your ass back and forth and spread your legs a little, your green high-heeled shoes carelessly kicking the pillows off the bed.

"I'm sorry, Santa," you mewl rapturously. "I promise I didn't let myself come!"

I transfer the belt to my left hand and slide my ice-cold fingers between your legs, easing them under the soaked crotch of the G-string to feel your pussy. You gasp as two of my freezing fingers open your cunt and feel the heat there.

"You got yourself good and wet, though, didn't you?"

"All ready for Santa," you say with husky excitement.

The second that saucy line is out of your mouth, I'm back on you, the heavy belt rising and falling rapidly as you writhe in my lap. Little cries of dismay erupt from your green-glossed lips as you clutch at my thighs and rub your breasts against my steadily hardening cock. I redden your bottom until it contrasts festively with the green garters and the green lace tops of your stockings. Then I reach down and pick up the new vibrator from where it lies on the floor.

"Show Santa how you got yourself in trouble," I growl, seizing your hand and wrapping it around the vibrator's handle. I click the toy on to HIGH, knowing full well that you likely would prefer the low setting. But you don't hesitate. Obediently, you reach down with your green-nailed fingers and pluck your G-string out of the way, pressing the head of the vibe to your clit. You shriek immediately, but when you try to pull away I grab your hand and force the vibrator more firmly against your clit—which makes you shudder all over and lose your grip on the G-string. I thoughtfully yank it up. It's cheap fabric; it tears without a sound and the soaked triangle of fabric falls uselessly between your thighs, exposing your pussy.

"Show Santa what you did," I growl. "Show Santa how you've been naughty. While I tan your elf ass."

You press the vibrator even harder against your clit, bending your knees so you can lift your ass high into the air and show me everything. I raise my hand and bring the belt down across your elfin ass once again, harder this time. You squeal and I grab your hair, molding your body, pushing you back on the bed until you're doubled over, ass still exposed but face in my crotch. You've got one free hand, and you put it to good use, unbuttoning the fly of the cheap costume and reaching in for my cock.

You find it unfettered by underwear, and in an instant you've got it in your mouth, even as I strap you harder. You moan softly, a muffled sound of pleasure as you mount toward orgasm, the vibrator's hum rhythmically stifled by the press of your clit against the head. You wrap your fingers around the shaft of my cock to steady it as you bob up and down, occasionally pausing to look up at me. You want to make sure Santa likes what you're doing.

Half of me expects to see green contact lenses hovering in your eyes, but when I don't, I bring the belt down swiftly and your head returns to my cock and bobs even faster. I can tell you're close; your tongue strokes up and down my shaft go crazy, unfocused, and confused, as your coordination is assaulted by the approach of your orgasm. A swift blow with the belt across your upper thighs brings your focus back, and you suck my cock expertly as your ass, pushed so high your back must hurt, humps desperately onto the vibrator.

You can't keep sucking me when you finally come; my cock pops free of your mouth and your lips part wide in a big O as a thunderous moan explodes from deep inside you. You keep stroking, though, your hand clutching the shaft of my cock as I strap you across the ass unexpectedly, which only serves to heighten your climax, and you take the head of my cock back into your mouth. You keep stroking as I groan in orgasm, filling your mouth as I give you three more quick strokes and savor the shudder through your body that signals the final pulsing sensations of your orgasm. As I finish coming, you sink down, sprawling across the bed, now only your head in my lap, your mouth still on my cock, your legs spread wide and the vibrator still humming between them until I reach down to turn it off.

You roll onto your back and look up at me, pleased and hungry like the naughty elf you are. Your breasts have popped out of the push-up bra, your nipples now evident— ringed with green niobium jewelry.

"There are more presents under the tree," I tell you. "But I think you've been too naughty to have them."

You wriggle your way up to a kneeling position on the bed, putting your arms around me. "I've got the only present I care about, Santa."

My arm curves around you and I cup your pussy, feeling its moisture as I stroke your slit. You clutch me more tightly and bite my neck, growling softly.

"In that case," I say, "you haven't been naughty enough. But we'll keep working on it."

Rapt
Saskia Walker

For a split second, I thought it was snowing. But no, it was
rain, as usual. The snow never comes to England much before January, which is just as well because as a nation we
don't know how to deal with it, and right now I didn't want
to be stuck in gridlock traffic due to an unexpected flurry of
snow on Christmas Eve. I braced myself for the cold drizzle
and stepped out of the Heathrow European arrivals terminal,
wondering how long I'd have to wait for a taxi.

As I darted toward the taxi rank, I threw a filthy look
down at the laptop bag I had in one hand and the bulging gift
bags in the other. Who sent their journalists on long distance
assignments on Christmas Eve? Only my boss! And because I
hadn't been organized enough to get the presents sorted and
delivered the weekend before, they'd had to come with me
on the trip. All I wanted to do was go back to my apartment,

get out of my heels and my business suit, and have a nice long bath……and some serious sexual relief. After an entire afternoon interviewing Dita, the enthusiastic designer for an Amsterdam sex toy company, I really needed some self-indulgent time of my own. Instead, I had to get a cab straight to my sister's townhouse in Hampstead Heath, where the entire family would be waiting to begin the Christmas celebrations. I sighed, deep and long.

The last few stragglers in the taxi queue were getting into London's trademark big black cabs, and as the next one pulled up, I calculated that this one was mine. I ran to the nearest door and threw my bags in on the floor, thanking my lucky stars.

"Oh no," I muttered, when the door on the other side sprang open and a briefcase and gift bags not dissimilar to my own were thrown in.

"Oh yes," my challenger said, ducking his head inside and grinning across the back of the cab at me. Wow, he was sexy. He waggled one eyebrow at me suggestively. "And I thought we British were supposed to be so good at queuing."

He'd won the argument outright with that remark.

"I'm really sorry, I didn't see you in the queue. I thought everyone had gone."

He glanced at the driver who was watching over his shoulder, waiting for us to sort it out between ourselves, and then he stepped up into the cab, eyeing me as he did so. I couldn't take my eyes off him either; the urgent hunger of a woman in heat beat out a demanding rhythm in the pit of my belly. I watched him unbutton his jacket and spread his long legs across the roomy floor of the cab, taking full advantage of the space. He was well built, with a rich, languorous sensuality in his expression, like a lion on the prowl. He rested one elbow against the seat, angling his body toward me. The look in his eyes was making me hot; he was staring at me with barefaced speculation. I suddenly realized that I was standing with my hands still on the frame of the door, one stacked heel inside the cab poised to climb in, my coat open and flashing him not only a good length of leg, but a bird's-eye view of my cleavage.

"Where are you headed, perhaps we can share?"

"Hampstead Heath," I mumbled. Looking behind the cab, I saw that no other taxis had joined the rank, but a new procession of weary travelers were spilling out of the terminal and headed our way.

"In that case, let's share, it's on my way." He opened his hand toward me in a friendly, beckoning gesture. I didn't have a lot of choice; I was already late. Besides, it wasn't every day a sexy guy like that offered to share a ride. In fact, it was practically unheard of in the city. I felt like Santa had come early. Perhaps the holiday spirit was mellowing us. Perhaps it was those brandies I'd had on the flight. Perhaps it was that hunger inside me, taking me over, making me throw caution to the wind. Whatever the reason, I took the hand he offered, sliding into the seat next to him with a grateful smile.

"Where to?" the driver asked, shouting over the blaring radio, then nodding as I gave the address. As he pulled away, he shut the window between him and us and turned his radio even louder.

"We obviously distracted him from his boxing match," the man beside me said. I shrugged at his remark, laughing as the cab lurched and flung me into place on the seat next to him. I caught a breath of his aftershave as I dipped in against him, my hip landing against his thigh as I settled into the seat, my body almost in his arms.

"Sorry," I whispered, straightening up.

"Don't apologize, I enjoyed it," he replied, and gave me the most devastating smile. We were alone in the gloomy interior of the cab and he was sending out very inviting signals. The prospect of being trapped in gridlock was suddenly a whole lot more appealing.

The lights from the underground pickup lane flashed by, racing across his face as he smiled over at me. It was going to take a while to get to my destination, and I wasn't in any rush. He was dark and ruggedly good-looking, and he had the most devilish expression in his eyes. His proximity and boldness, together with the solid rumble of the engine vibrating along the floor and up through my body, brought about a new rush of thoughts about physical pleasure.

The cab whisked out of the terminal area, through the Heathrow underpass and into the night. I was just settling down when, on the first roundabout, my gift bag tipped over and I snatched at it as the contents spilled over the floor.

"Let me help," he said, leaning over to pick up the various packages that had rolled out onto the floor of the cab.

"Thanks." I smiled at him. We were millimeters apart, swaying into each other with the rhythm of the cab. He lifted the packages into the bag that I was holding open. His hand brushed against mine, sending a frisson of electricity darting beneath my skin.

"Someone is going to be getting to unwrap lots of goodies," he commented, as he put the packages back into the bag. He wasn't, however, looking at the gifts, he was looking pointedly at my cleavage, and he wasn't attempting to hide the fact.

"Do you always come on to women who try to steal your cabs?"

If he was going to flirt, then I was up for it. It was the little devil that lived in my head; he made me naughty.

"Only if they are very attractive brunettes."

Right backatcha, huh. He had my full attention. Not to mention the fact that I was very flattered by his comment.

"This one isn't wrapped, does that means it's for you?"

I dragged my eyes off his face and looked at the box in his hand. I swallowed hard and stared, in absolute astonishment. I couldn't quite believe it. He was holding a sex toy in his hand—a clit sucker! The lurid name and depiction on the label made that plain enough. *Where the hell had that come from?* I suddenly realized that Dita must have slipped it into my bag as I was leaving the design studio. What should I say: deny knowledge of it and look like a furtive, gauche idiot, or brazen it out as nonchalantly as I could? I remembered Dita grinning at me as she waved me off, and I knew what a woman like Dita would have done.

"A girl has to treat herself sometimes, you know." I managed to get the words out, and then went to grab the box off him, hoping that he wouldn't spot me blushing in the gloomy interior of the cab.

"Oh no," he said, moving his hand out of my reach. "I've never seen one of these before, and you obviously know what it's all about, so why don't you give this poor innocent guy here a demo?"

"A demo," I repeated, aghast. He didn't look innocent at all; he knew exactly what he was doing.

"Yes, you know, show me how it works, I'm fascinated."

He was serious. He offered me the box. A deep pang of longing made itself known between my thighs. I'd been wired all day, watching Dita handle the demo models with such expertise; describing the pleasures they would give. My attention had been rapt. I hadn't even bothered to make notes for my feature; every word and image was emblazoned on my mind. And now there was a provocative man beside me suggesting that I show *him* what it was all about. My body was on fire with arousal.

I remembered what Dita had said about the toy. I could demo it just as she had, couldn't I? It was the little devil that lived in my head again, urging me to be naughty.

I took the box and peeled off the plastic wrapper. I tried to look as if I knew what I was doing, remembering each move Dita had made. The cab suddenly lurched around a corner as I opened the lid, and the contents slid out onto my lap. I looked down at the cylinder and its pump-head attachment. My hands didn't feel altogether steady. Could I really pull it off?

"Wow," he commented. "This all looks very technical."

"Yes, willing mouths are much simpler." *Oh no!* The words were out before I'd even thought it through. His eyebrows lifted, his expression very amused. "I mean…""

"You don't need to explain. I understand you perfectly…and I agree. But let's not spoil the unwrapping of your present."

I was overwhelmed with a heady cocktail of arousal and self-awareness, and I don't know if that remark helped or made things worse for me. But I was determined. I wanted him to know I was a sophisticated, independent woman, not a blushing idiot. I grasped at the plastic covering on the suction pump head and pulled it off, revealing the clit sucker in all its pink-jelly-rubber glory. Before he could say another word, I picked up the cylinder and screwed the pieces together. I switched it on, held it up, and then—and only then—dared to look back at him. The clit sucker made an insinuating purring sound between us, its movement subtle but just visible under the passing streetlights. And now it was his attention that was rapt, just as mine had been when I'd first seen it.

He looked back at me, quizzically.

"There you go. Once it makes contact, it creates a seal. The suction rate is variable," I demonstrated, notching it up and back down," so you can go for fast pleasure or…draw it out for as long as you can stand it." I felt like I was telling this guy my innermost secrets and desires, somehow, and yet I wasn't. This was me being brave; this was me daring to be as brave as Dita. Maybe it was the way he looked at me. His eyes were burning with keen intensity. Maybe it was the fact I was horny as fuck, and I had a willing man and a fascinating gadget at hand.

"I take it this means you're single?"

"What?" *How did he know that?*

"If you bought yourself the toy?" He gave a suggestive smile.

He was fishing for information. "Oh, right, yes actually." I nodded.

He reached over and traced one hand down my neck, touching the surface of my skin ever so lightly. It was like slow, delicious torture, and yet I felt that he knew exactly what effect it was having on me.

"And you look like you're more than ready to try your new toy; I can see that you're very aroused." His hand dropped down and he ran his fingertips across my breasts, where my nipples stood like totems under my soft cashmere shirt.

"Yes, I am." I blurted it out, unable to stop myself. But it felt so good to say it aloud. I bit my bottom lip, to stop myself from whimpering loudly as well. "This is quite an arousing situation we find ourselves in, is it not?" It was my turn to fix him with a questioning gaze. He nodded. He was looking so damned interested. That sent my breathing right out of whack.

"In that case…" He leaned forward and planted a kiss right in my cleavage. The subtle but direct touch sent a hot flare of desire soaring through me. "Why not give me the full, X-rated demo," he whispered, raising his head. "I can see that you want to. It is Christmas, after all." The humidity level between my thighs hit the top of the scale. In that moment I was convinced I'd die if I didn't get some action. Could I really do it? *Yes,* my body roared. I felt his hand stroke up and over my thigh, easing under the hem of my short skirt with purpose. He groaned in approval when he exposed my stocking tops.

"What about the driver?" I asked, wondering if it would even be possible for me to stop following where this was headed; I was so fueled up.

"He's far too interested in the boxing to notice what we're up to." I nodded. "Just tell me to stop, and I will," he whispered, as his fingers scratched over the scrap of sheer lace panties between him and my lusting sex. He nodded his head at the clit sucker, which I still held aloft in one hand.

"It needs lubricant," I mumbled and then watched in awe as he took the gadget off me, dipped his head toward the pink head, and ran his tongue back and forth inside it, right where it was perfectly shaped to fit snugly over the clit. That sight was enough to drive any woman wild! Before I knew what I was doing, I was moving my hips, rubbing my pussy against his hand. I took the clit sucker back from him and hit the switch, indicating it was all stations *go*. My coat fell down off my shoulders and my legs moved apart, automatically. He eased my skirt right up and my panties down to my knees.

"Show me," he whispered, leaning over my sprawled hips.

Somehow my hands went into autopilot and I moved the clit sucker into position, the fingers of my free hand opening me up, sliding down either side of my swollen clit.

When I felt the first tug of the sucker on my sensitive, aroused flesh, I nearly lifted off the seat. The contact was so specific; it sent wild torrents of pleasure roaring through me. My back arched, my body leeched to the breathtaking sensations. This little beauty was going to give orgasm on demand! Glancing down, I saw that the man was watching me, fascinated, his hand stroking my thigh soothingly. I was so turned on by him, and by the situation, I was about to come at any moment.

"That looks so good," I head him murmur. I opened my legs wider, and watched as his hand moved closer to my heat. *Where had this exhibitionist streak come from?* Was I really doing this, masturbating in front of a complete stranger in a cab? *Yes*, I was, and it felt thoroughly debauched, dirty and yet…so right! Even as the thought crossed my mind, I felt his finger slide inside me, stroking against the hot, slippery surface of my sex, hard and inquisitive. And then it was too much and I was bucking and whimpering, my clit thrumming and my sex clenching as a hot tide of release washed over me.

When I surfaced, I could hear my own raspy breathing, the sound of the engine in the background and a very distant boxing commentary. He kissed my mouth then, and I melted all over again.

"We're almost there," he said, as he turned from me and peered through the fogged window.

"But, I…" I tried to focus, my eyes on the very attractive

bulge at his groin. We were almost there, and I had wanted to repay his favor. I wanted to give him head, right there and then.

His eyes were darting and suggestive. "I'll be thinking about how hot you looked just now all night long…when I'm alone in my bed." Yes, I understood that, and I was glad, and I pictured him with his hand on his cock. Oh yes, I wanted to see that. "Would you like to do this again?" he added.

"What, attempt to steal your cab?" I replied, mischievously, as I hurriedly pulled my clothes into place. I snatched the clit sucker off the seat and shoved it into my coat pocket.

"I prefer to think of it as sharing a very pleasurable *ride*, don't you?" He reached into his inner jacket pocket and handed me a business card. His name was Max, Max Lane. And I wanted him. He had touched me, but so fleetingly. I wanted heavy action, bodies rolling together, and furious, sweaty, full-on, pumping 'n' grinding sex. *But it's only Christmas Eve*, my little devil reminded me. *Yes,* I agreed, the holiday season was only just beginning. There was plenty of time for more fun and games.

I nodded, smiling at the card, then slid it into my coat pocket alongside the clit sucker. "And I would like to do it again, Mr. Max Lane…. I like to get out of the house by myself for a while on Christmas Day, do you?"

"That does sound good." We exchanged looks over the agreement, both of us smiling. "I saw you running over and I couldn't believe it when you got into my cab. I'd been expecting another uneventful family Christmas at my sister's place."

"Me, too," I said and pulled him in for another kiss. His mouth was gorgeous, sensitive and aware. I wanted more of it.

The noise of the driver's window sliding open and a renewed sports commentary on full volume interrupted us. We had arrived. I pulled away and grabbed my bags, jumping out of the cab.

"I'll take care of the fare," Max said, when I opened my bag for cash.

"In that case, I'll pay the next time we share a ride."

I was light headed, dizzy with pleasure. Something about him had made me feel extraordinarily uninhibited and mischievous, and the mood wasn't fading. I was just about to suggest a rendezvous time for the next day when a loud cough drew us back from our mutual reverie.

"Normally I'd charge extra for a Christmas Eve pickup," the taxi driver announced, deadpan. "But I guess I'll have to give you two a discount…on account of the show."

My mouth dropped open.

Max chuckled, breaking the sudden rush of embarrassment I felt. What the hell, it was too late to worry about it now. Max pulled the door closed after me, then rolled down the window. "Call me soon," he shouted, as the taxi pulled away.

"Tomorrow!" I answered, waving, as I realized I hadn't even told him my name. The taxi disappeared into two bright dots on the dark horizon, and I noticed that the rain had stopped. Turning away, I could see the Christmas lights in my sister's window and figures moving inside the house. The muted sound of the Christmas hit parade emerged from the house. I felt a whole lot more ready for this. Ready for this evening, and whatever other magic gifts the season brought me to unwrap.

Unwrapped
Ayre Riley

On Christmas Eve, I worked slowly to get myself ready. I knew I had plenty of time. West was playing with his band at a local holiday party, and he wouldn't be home until a bit after midnight. I'd told him that I wasn't in the mood for a party, but that wasn't the truth at all. I was *definitely* in the mood for a party—but only for a party of two, and by the time he returned home, I would be fully prepared.

Standing in front of my vanity, I did my makeup first, using black mascara to emphasize my big, brown eyes before adding a glossy ruby lipstick. My curly brown hair was up on my head, a few sexy strands falling free around my face. I looked taller with my hair like that, and exotic. That was my goal—I did not want to appear like West's regular girlfriend with the standard ponytail and all-natural looking makeup. I wanted to transform myself into someone festive and magical, a glittery sex angel ready to make his kinkiest Christmas wishes come true.

For clothes, I had chosen a sheer black teddy trimmed with satin and a matching G-string. On top of the naughty knickers, I buckled a sleek leather harness with a brand-new cock. I wasn't going for an androgynous appearance, or turning myself into a man who was hot to fuck my beau. For this erotic event, I simply wanted to be West's sexy girlfriend— but one who sported a cock as long and hard as West had ever dreamed about. And I knew all about those dreams. Visions of sugarplums didn't dance in my man's head. X-rated images of me with a strap-on were what gave West the most pleasure in bed.

My heels were high and trimmed with tiny silver bells, so that I jingled when I walked. I strode around the apartment, feeling the arousal build inside of me as I made my way from room to room. This was going to be amazing, an evening to top all others. I lit twisted ivory candles on the mantle, then checked the clock in the center. Nearly time! I hoped he wouldn't be too late. I was as excited as a little kid waiting for Santa Claus.

When I heard his key in the lock, I slid into the gold lamé robe that was my final touch for the festive outfit. I wrapped the cord tightly around my slim waist, but it did nothing to hide the sexy bulge beneath. That was fine. I wanted West to see that bulge. I wanted him to understand. I faced away from the door, acting as if I were straightening the Christmas stockings.

"Hey, baby," West said, coming up behind me and grabbing me in his standard bear-hug embrace. "Why are you all dolled up?"

I turned to face him, and I could see the surprise in his

eyes when he felt my own surprise against his thigh.

"It's Christmas," I told him. "See? It's after midnight." I motioned to the mantle clock. "I wanted to give you your present now."

"My present—?" he stammered as I took one of his big hands and placed it on the front of my robe. He knew what to do, even if he couldn't fully speak. His hand stroked my cock through the glittery fabric, and I watched him swallow hard.

"My present," he said again, his voice no longer holding a questioning tone. It was clear to me that he realized what I had in store.

"You've been such a good boy this year," I grinned at him. "Santa prepared a special gift for you."

"Special—" he repeated as I pushed him back onto the sofa and watched him stumble into a sitting position among our many overstuffed pillows. His eyes were wide open with a combination of wonder and lust. I could tell that my plans were working, and I felt an added jolt of confidence burst through me. West was definitely getting more and more aroused, almost in spite of himself.

I walked with my jingling stride back to the mantle where the stockings had been hung with care, and I pulled out a package decoratively wrapped in silver and gold. I handed it to my man, but he just sat there, staring at me.

"Open it," I instructed, realizing that I was going to have to lead him through all of the evening's events. Still unsure, West looked down at the box in his hands, then back at me, and then finally he tore into the wrapping and ripped off the box top, quickly revealing a pair of fur-lined cuffs.

"Take off your clothes," I told him next. "Everything but your boxers."

West didn't need any additional prompting. He stripped

off his boots, slacks, shirt, and blazer, and then immediately held his wrists in front of him. He was nervous; I could tell. But he was excited, too. That much was obvious from the way his green eyes watched every motion I made. I cuffed him easily, then returned to my stockings filled with tricks. From the second one, I pulled out another package.

"You'll have to unwrap that," he said wryly, indicating his cuffed wrists. While he watched, I shredded the shiny paper to reveal a large bottle of expensive lube. I saw West's dark eyes grow wide.

"Are you ready for your big present?" I asked.

He nodded slowly.

"I'll unwrap it for you," I told him kindly, untying the cord on my robe and letting it fall open. West groaned when he saw my cock. He'd felt its presence, but seeing it right there, standing away from my body like that, made him understand how real this evening was.

"All right, naughty boy," I murmured to him. "Now, it's time for me to unwrap *my* present." I worked his boxers down bit by bit, watching excitedly as his erection sprang free. Then I locked his cock between my full lips and gave him a few slow sucks. West groaned appreciatively, settling back into our deep sofa as I worked him. I took my time, licking his shaft up and down before turning my attention to his balls. I cradled each one in my mouth, then cupped both together between my lips and flicked my tongue against them. West started to breathe faster and faster as I played with him, and he set his handcuffed wrists against the back of my head, helping me set the rhythm.

"Oh, Alex," he whispered. "Alexandra. That feels so good."

"It's going to feel even better," I assured him. "Now, roll over for me, West."

He didn't move. I could tell that he wanted to, but he was scared.

"Don't worry," I assured him. "I know exactly how to take care of you." As if calmed by my words, he quietly rolled over, knees on the floor, ass toward me, elbows bent, and cuffed wrists near his face. I got the bottle of lube and poured a generous amount into the palm of my hand. Slowly and gently I readied him for my toy, rubbing my fingers between his asscheeks and then in delicious circles around his opening. West lifted his hips each time I touched his anus, and when I put one hand beneath him to feel his cock, he was already dripping pre-come.

Recalling how I sometimes felt being in the same position, I took my time. I massaged and teased, taunting him with little dips of my fingertips inside his ass until he couldn't stand it any longer.

"Please," he begged me. "Please, baby—"

I knew he was ready, and I was definitely ready, so I parted the cheeks of his ass and slid just the head of the cock forward. He groaned and turned his head to the side. I saw that his eyes were shut tight. I ruffled his blond hair lightly, reminding him that this was me, his loving girlfriend—that he didn't need to hide behind closed lids. Then I pushed forward a bit more with my hips, sliding the cock deeper inside him. Or, rather, *my* cock deeper. I felt as if I'd joined with the toy, become one with the synthetic object.

I fucked West the same way I liked him to fuck me, long and slow at first, going in a bit deeper with each thrust. Then, as I got into the groove, I worked him a bit harder, gripping on to his hips for leverage as I took him. West started to make noises that I'd never heard from him before. Low, harsh grunts that let me know how turned on he was. He panted with each thrust forward, and groaned as I pulled back out.

"I'm going to—" he said, his voice a husky whisper.

"Not yet," I insisted, and now I reached under his body, gripped and started to milk his cock in time with the ass-fucking I was giving him. In and out, stroke and hold. I made him shudder all over as he tried desperately to reign himself in.

As I fucked him, I thought about how West had confessed this fantasy to me. Late one night after Thanksgiving, we'd curled around each other and revealed our deepest secrets. It had felt as if he'd unwrapped his inner soul for me, showing me who he was for real. Now, in the middle of the living room, amidst scraps of glittering wrapping paper, we were as naked for each other as we could possibly be, completely and utterly unwrapped.

When I could tell he was at his very limit, I said, "All right, baby—" and he came in great shivering gasps, bucking and shooting as I jacked him off.

We lay there together, connected, until our breathing grew steady once again. Then I pulled out and tucked myself back into my robe, tying it shut but leaving my cock in place.

"So Santa arranged for all of this?" He smiled at me as I unlocked the cuffs.

"Yes," I nodded. "All the way from the North Pole. Or, rather, San Francisco. I ordered it from an adorably kinky mail-order catalog."

"Well, Santa can always use a little extra help," West grinned, wrapping me tightly in his arms.

Last-Minute Shopping
Rachel Kramer Bussel

The only thing my boyfriend really wanted for Christmas was the new Vice City game, and I, having had a particularly busy December, hadn't had a proper chance to shop for him. So as I set out desperately on the evening of December 24, I found myself going from store to store, only to be told at each and every one that they had *just* sold the last one that day. Behind their fake pity was a knowing and critical glare, judging me for leaving my shopping until the very last minute. It's not like I was the only one! There were hordes of pushy shoppers practically knocking me over to get to the newest GameBoy or iPod, all in the relentless pursuit of more and more things to crowd their already filled-to-the-brim houses. This was the real reason I dreaded Christmas shopping in the first place.

I had tried to do it earlier, even tried to shop online, to no avail. I got stuck waiting for pages to load or finding that "in stock" really meant "may be in stock, we're not sure, check back with us next week." I figured that the stores would be able to anticipate the demand for such a popular item and have plenty on hand. Now that I had promised Jim that this would be his gift from me, after ascertaining that this was really, truly, exactly what he wanted and any substitute just wouldn't do, I might as well mark BAD GIRLFRIEND across my forehead in indelible ink if I didn't have it for him on Christmas Day.

Finally, as the time neared eight, I approached one dimly lit storefront—it seemed to carry every kind of electronic paraphernalia imaginable, the windows a jumble of cameras and computers, gadgets and yes, the occasional video game. I tried the door and found it locked, but knocked gingerly anyway—at this point I didn't have anything to lose. Finally, after a few minutes of knocking and grating my knuckles against the door, standing and shivering in the icy cold air, I saw a man appear from the back of the store. And by *man,* I don't mean some generic clerk—old and dusty as his merchandise, wearing an ancient moth-eaten sweater and looking like a doddering uncle, or an unfriendly, snarling, acne-scarred teenager. No, this one was all M-A-N, big, burly, and strapping, as he opened the door and ushered me inside.

And even though the door had been locked, he didn't look the least bit perturbed to be roused so late on Christmas Eve; in fact, from the appraising look on his face and the kind crinkle to his eyes, I'd almost have thought he'd been expecting me. His smile gave me a tingling sensation all over. I shook my head to remind myself that I was here to get a present for Jim, and I stepped inside away from the cold before he could deny me the opportunity. My exhaustion caused me to blurt out exactly what I needed.

"Hi, I know it's Christmas Eve and everything, believe me, but I'm looking for the latest Vice City game, and I've been to almost every store in town and nobody seems to have it and I'm really, really desperate. I must find that game for my boyfriend or he will absolutely kill me!" I said it all in a great rush of breath, afraid he might stop listening to me if I paused. He just smiled that lazy, sexy smile at me.

"Let's see what we can do to help you out," he said, with none of the judgmental bullshit I'd had to deal with all afternoon. "You know," he added kindly, "good things come to those who wait." As he led me toward the stockroom, my eyes were magnetically drawn to the way his dark blue jeans clung to his tight ass, which looked more enticing with each step. I tried to listen to what he was saying but it wasn't easy; after pushy, whiny, annoying salespeople lecturing me all day, here he was—hunky, handsome, and helpful!

My heart beat faster with each step. I was finally within reach of the goal that I'd been sure only an hour before was hopeless. I'd been certain I would have to find a way to break it to Jim that the gift I had promised him, *assured* him he didn't have to get for himself, wouldn't be in his hot little hands the minute the clock struck midnight on Christmas Eve. I knew that he'd recover well—he always does—but I didn't want to disappoint him. I wasn't even sure if pulling out my most unusual sex tricks would work to counter his disappointment. Now that there was a chance I was going to get the gift, I felt a strange mixture of relief, arousal, and uncertainty at this unexpected turn of events.

I snapped back to the present as I found myself facing shelf after shelf packed with video games. The man started telling me what each one was. I didn't want to be rude and interrupt him to explain that there was only one game I was interested in. Just as he was pointing with one hand to the farthest reaches of the store, the games piled so high they almost touched the ceiling, I felt him grab my hand with his other and rub it along the front of his jeans. And let me tell you—*he* was just as excited about this Vice City game as I was. His cock felt huge, and I told myself that I couldn't really politely move away, and besides, it was *his* hand pressing mine along his hardness. I was just an innocent last-minute shopper. He continued to pontificate about the various games he offered and why the latest Vice City was so wonderful and how he was sure my boyfriend would love it—but when he got to that last line, his fingers ever so slowly and quietly began to unzip his jeans so that now my fingers were placed against something even firmer and hotter.

He was wearing briefs, but he may as well not have been, because I could feel everything beneath them. I was starting to lose interest in the game I was after and become more interested in the unspoken game my mysterious salesman and I were playing. It was like chicken—who would be the first to step away, to call a halt to this insane mating dance? And yet I couldn't go first; now it was no longer about the present, but about the firm promise of the cock I held in my hand, that responded to every minuscule movement of my fingers. I stayed next to him as he walked (slowly) to get a ladder, and then followed him up the ladder as he got the game down from the very top shelf, almost toppling a stack of boxes and ourselves in the process. When he started back down the ladder, I stayed where I was, looking up at him, my personal Christmas hero, and he slowly eased himself around to face me.

I balanced myself while I undid his belt buckle, knowing that our tense positioning on the ladder only made this more exciting. Then I pulled him toward me and started licking him through the white cotton, lightly running my teeth over his underwear-clad cock, marveling at how he seemed to get bigger by the second. I leaned forward and with the utmost care for our delicate placement, pushed his jeans down and peeled back the waistband of his underwear to reveal my reward—his hard, thick, glorious cock, standing there waiting to be devoured. And devour it I did, slowly guiding it into my already salivating mouth, making sure not to move any more than necessary. We could have descended the ladder and found a cozy spot in the office, but that would have made this too deliberate, and I couldn't think about my true reason for shopping here or what he was holding in his hands if I wanted to enjoy the way his cock filled my entire mouth, the way it tickled the back of my throat and made me want to keep it inside me forever. I licked my way all around his cock, exploring every wet inch of it, wrapping my fist around its meatiness and plunging it into my mouth. I could feel my panties dampening with each slide of his cock into my mouth—I'm a sucker for a killer blowjob—and I moved slightly so the heel of my shoe pressed up against my pussy, teasing me further.

Finally, when he could stand it no longer, he yelled "Down," in a voice I knew I had to obey if I didn't want to fall off the ladder. We scrambled down and I plunged my mouth right back where it had been, and he slammed into me, coming in a hot salty burst that I immediately swallowed. I kept him in my mouth for a few moments longer, not wanting to break the spell. When I finally emerged from the cocoon of his cock, I straightened up and looked at the ground, then finally flicked my eyes toward him. I could tell he wanted to smile, to invite me into his office, offer me some champagne, maybe invite me home, but he didn't. He simply held the game out to me, the garish cartoon figures on the box peering out at me, waiting for the thrill rides my boyfriend would be sure to take them on.

"For you," he said, "on the house."

It was a crazy, wild, surprising thing for me to have done, and of course now I had to almost ruin it all by wanting to kiss and hug this gorgeous hunk. Instead, I pressed a kiss against my fingertips, then gingerly placed them against his lips. If I'd been another type of girl, one who did this type of thing on a regular basis, I would have winked, but I'm not, so I didn't. Instead I gathered my coat and delicately walked out of the store, barely feeling the cold as I made my way to my car, hastily wrapped the present, and drove home in a daze.

I got back around ten, in time to indulge in some eggnog and see the look of happiness on Jim's face as he tore open his present and joyfully went over to the television and started playing his new game. I didn't ruin his holiday by telling him exactly how I'd acquired the gift.

Some things—especially when they involve last-minute shopping—are best kept to yourself.

Beneath the Mistletoe
Michelle Houston

Lisa leaned against the wall, watching as everyone at the annual office Christmas party danced and mingled with others they would normally have nothing to do with. The VP of marketing was chatting about his new baby's teething and diaper rash with the janitor, and since he was well in his cups, Lisa doubted he even noticed who it was he was talking to.

She watched as the president of the company wandered around in his baggy Santa suit, ho-ho-humbugging as he passed out the yearly bonus checks. Yep, it was another typical Christmas party: a lot of forced jollity and merriment, drunken conversations, and a general waste of time.

Lisa was mentally debating how much longer she was going to have to stick around and suffer this farce of a party, when two soft hands covered her eyes and a set of breasts settled against her back. Inhaling slightly, she smiled as she recognized her lover's perfume.

"Guess who?" her petite sweetheart whispered.

"Well, I know it isn't Santa, since he was just across the room. Mrs. Claus maybe, come to save my evening?"

A seductive giggle was followed by a "No."

"Hum, maybe an adventurous elf? Wait, I know, you're a Santa imposter, right?"

Lisa could feel her lover, Janis, shift behind her, then a breathy whispering in her ear, "No, silly, I'm the woman who is going to take you home, dress up in my satin naughty Santa outfit, and fuck you senseless beneath the Christmas tree."

As the hands moved from her eyes, Lisa turned so that she faced Janis. "That sounds like the best Christmas gift a girl could ask for. Unfortunately, I was chosen to stay and clean up, since I'm supposedly one of the 'swinging singles.' "

Red rouged lips curved into a truly gorgeous pout. Even after two years together, Lisa still couldn't get over how sinful her lover's lips were.

"Well then, Ms. Responsible, I guess I'll simply have to kidnap you for a bit and take you back to your office to take some clerical dictation. Or since you're a woman, some clitation." Her eyes twinkled with the joy of the season, naughty thoughts, and a bit too much spiked eggnog.

Clasping Lisa's hand in hers, Janis pulled her gently away from the rowdy party and down the hall to her office.

Once they were inside with the door safely locked, Janis curled herself around Lisa and began to kiss her. Lisa grasped her lover's ass and pulled the petite blonde up against her.

Silently thanking her luck that her lover was so flexible, she slid to her knees on the plush carpet and pulled Janis down with her. Moving back for a moment was like trying to get away from a horny octopus, but somehow Lisa managed it. Although she was breathing hard, her hands were steady as she began unbuttoning her blouse and pulling it free from her slacks.

Since Janis was wearing a barely-there skirt outfit, she merely parted her legs and pulled her skirt up to her waist, baring her smooth-shaven and pantyless flesh to view. Lisa's eyes almost crossed in lust. Flushed a dark red and glistening with her sweet juices, Janis's pussy was adorned with a tiny stalk of mistletoe attached to her clit ring.

"Remember to pay close attention to what's beneath the mistletoe, baby," Janis whispered as she threaded her fingers through Lisa's hair. Pulling the brunette down to her, Janis ground her wet core against her lover's tongue.

Her nose brushing against the white and green sign of the season, Lisa inhaled her lover's delicious scent as she savored the feast before her. This was Lisa's favorite holiday meal. She thrust her tongue in and out of her lover, listening to the blonde whimper for more. As Janis's passion mounted, whimpers became moans and then turned into soft screams. Listening to the sounds, feeling the grinding and bucking beneath her, Lisa knew the exact moment to thrust two fingers into Janis's pussy and hold on for the ride.

Screaming her pleasure, Janis twisted and thrust into her lover's face, her sweet juices coating her thighs.

As she lay on the carpet gasping for breath, her body trembling, Janis opened her eyes to watch her beloved disrobe and come to kneel at her side. Holding the mistletoe up where Janis could see it, Lisa repeated, "Pay close attention to what's beneath the mistletoe," then placed it between her own nether lips and leaned back. Smiling, Janis was only too happy to return the favor.

By the time they returned to the party, almost everyone had gone home, and those unlucky enough to be stuck cleaning up either didn't notice, or simply chose not to comment on, the state of disarray both women were in. Working quickly, they soon had the room put back to rights and all of them headed off in their separate directions.

Linking arms with her slightly tipsy, and wickedly sensual Christmas elf, Lisa walked out into the moonlit December night and breathed deeply. Feeling the joy of the season flood her, she turned to her lover and placed a soft kiss upon her now rouge-less lips. Their holiday kiss was just as sweet, even without the mistletoe.

The Naughtiest Christmas
Xavier Acton

I was always naughty about Christmas presents—wrapped up under the tree, just sitting there taunting me—their contents *begged* to be guessed at, but I've never been a very good guesser. I am, however, great at wrapping things—and rewrapping. I know it's bad.

And Erica has always been good at surprising me.

She knew I'd sneak a peek at her Christmas goodies. She and I had only been together for three months, but since she lived with four roommates—and spent most of her time at my considerably more spacious top-floor apartment—we'd decided to put our gifts for each other under the tree at my place.

While I most caddishly opened Erica's gifts, she was stretching herself into unlikely postures at her yoga class, dreaming of how I was gently prying the tape from the big box, delicately peeling back its shimmering silver paper.

And staring with mixed horror and excitement at a box stuffed with gifts that would make the Marquis de Sade blush. And maybe even giggle.

First there was the ball gag, improbably large for Erica's small, pert mouth. It had a red ball and black leather straps that formed a harness, presumably meant to go around the head. The dog collar might have been intended merely as a post-punk fashion statement if it weren't for the shimmering silver chain with its clip and black grip, without a doubt meant to serve as a leash. Then there were the wrist and ankle cuffs, black leather and padded with sheepskin, clipped with metal carabiners to nylon-webbed straps.

I felt my cock hardening as I ran my fingers over the glistening black leather of Erica's gifts. We'd joked and teased about bondage, but never tried it—yet. Our three months together had been filled with frenzied sex, but the erotic charge we felt for each other was such that we'd rarely had time for experimentation. We were too busy fucking.

Now, though, I knew Erica was presenting me with just such an invitation. I imagined her as my prisoner: cuffed, gagged and stuffed full of dildo, my paddle leaving her gorgeous ass a bright-red, rosy hue. Just the thought of it was enough to make me touch my cock. I stroked myself to orgasm right there under the Christmas tree, with the vivid image of a decked-out Erica as my prisoner blazing in my head. I had to jerk off again just to get my hands steady enough to carefully rewrap the present so my naughty Santa wouldn't know for certain I had betrayed her confidence.

Despite two orgasms, I was still horny as hell when Erica dropped by after yoga. I seized her the second she arrived, and pressed my lips to hers while I wrestled her out of her leotard. Her body writhed against mine as I turned her around and pressed her against the door, then entered her from behind, still standing. The whole time I was picturing how she'd look in those delightful Christmas gifts. She came before I did and asked, later, about my sudden and uncontrollable passion.

"I guess I just missed you," I said guiltily.

The few weeks until Christmas flew by in a flurry of frenzied sex punctuated by the occasional gift buying. I was hotter than ever for Erica, knowing what a kinky, naughty secret she held. She made the most of her "secret," begging me to guess at the contents of the silver-wrapped box. I played my part as best I could, wondering out loud if she'd bought me that down comforter I'd liked or a new leather jacket.

She seemed gleeful each time I guessed wrong. "I think you're going to love it," she would say, then look worried. "I think."

"I'm sure I'll love it," I would say, trying hard not to be too obvious. "Is it a new set of curtains for the living room?"

"For God's sake," she said once. "How boring do you think I am?"

"Not very boring at all," I said with a smirk.

We decided to save our presents for each other until after the Christmas Eve visits to our nearby families and the Christmas Day rounds of our friends' houses with bottles of wine and gingerbread cookies. We came home late in the day on Christmas with Erica positively bouncing.

"I get to open my present first," she said. "After you open yours, we're not going to do anything except play with it. All right?"

"Awwww," I whined, just to be annoying. "Can't I open mine first? We'll want to play with yours, too."

I finally gave in, and Erica cheerfully shook the heavy box that held her laptop computer. When she opened it, she sat there stunned.

"Jesus Christ, it's too expensive," she said.

"It's the thought that counts," I answered blithely. "Besides, you can get into cybercrime to help get me out of the poorhouse. Now can I open my present?"

She put her arms around me and kissed me. "All right," she said. "But I'm not a hundred percent sure you're going to like it."

"Oh," I chortled, "I'm quite sure I will."

Her eyes narrowed in a moment of suspicion, but then she smiled broadly. "Open it!"

It felt strangely deconstructive unwrapping a present I'd wrapped in the style of Erica's wrapping, pretending to struggle with the little strips of tape and the big red bow. When I opened the box and feigned astonishment, I was only partly acting—because I could hardly believe I'd made it to Christmas without spilling the beans. And I was so fucking turned on knowing that Erica, at her request, was about to become my prisoner.

I held up the harness in shock and dangled the leash and the collar in front of her.

"You are one naughty fucking Santa," I said, starting to play the role. "You are a very, very, very bad Santa."

"Do you like it?" she asked sheepishly.

"I love it," I said. "This is such an incredible fucking turn-on. I've fantasized about this for as long as I can remember. I can't believe you bought all this stuff."

"But you like it?"

"Oh yes," I said. "I like it."

She nuzzled her face into my neck and whispered, "Want to play?"

"Absolutely," I told her.

"I've got another part of your present," she said. "I'm going to go change into it."

"Excellent," I told her. "I'll meet you in the bedroom."

Erica disappeared into the bathroom while I went to the bedroom and slipped out of my warm Christmas clothes. I turned down the lights, laid the naughty gifts out on the bed and lay down alongside them, as if in invitation. My cock was already hard anticipating the submission of my little slave.

Erica came out of the bathroom wearing the hottest piece of lingerie I'd ever seen on a woman. She wore a black push-up bra, accenting her small breasts, a black garter belt with fishnet stockings, and a black lace thong on over the garters. The sporty type, Erica usually favored relatively utilitarian cotton-spandex panties and sports bras. Seeing her decked out like the sluttiest femme in creation turned me on even more.

"Do you like it?" she asked nervously.

I climbed to my knees on the bed, naked, my cock standing out almost painfully hard. "Get over here," I told her.

She came for me, climbing onto the bed and pushing me onto my back. She kissed me hard, then trailed her tongue down my neck and nibbled my ear. Her hand disappeared into her lace thong and came back slick with her juices. She slid her fingers between my parted lips.

"See how fucking wet you make me?" she whimpered, pushing her fingers deep into my mouth. I nodded, sucking eagerly at her juices. Her voice tightened. "I'm going to make you pay for that."

"Um…okay," I said, confused.

"I'm going to make you pay for that, you little bitch."

"Excuse me?"

"Oh, you want to play hard to get?" she growled.

"Um," I said.

"Go on," she said, and her hand left my mouth only to return a moment later with the ball gag. "Play hard to get all you want. Mistress Erica's in charge tonight, slave, and you don't get to say no. Understand?"

Her finger was pointed right at the tip of my nose. My eyes felt like they were swimming uncontrollably in my head as I tried instinctively to focus on it. Finally, I looked up at her eyes, which were cold with fury. Her beautiful face held an expression I'd never seen before.

She grabbed my hair and made as if to slap my face.

"Get it?" she snarled.

It hadn't even been a tap, so light I could barely feel it, but it made the point and established the role. All my images of Erica bound like a submissive tart were swirled together in a mélange of shock and dismay—even as my cock throbbed harder than ever between my legs.

She slapped me again, barely a touch, just a whisper that told me she was in charge.

"Get it?"

"No," I sneered, looking at her with mock disgust. "I don't get it at all."

So she slapped me again, this time harder, hard enough that I could feel it, hard enough that my cheek warmed under the blow and sent a cascading flood of excitement down to my cock.

"I'll shut up that smart mouth," she said. "Then you won't mouth off any more."

Breathing hard, I nodded. "Yes, Mistress. You'll have to

gag me to keep me from mouthing off."

She laughed. "Oh, you'll mouth off later," she said. "You felt how wet I am." Then she popped the ball gag into my mouth and quickly and expertly cinched the black leather straps around my head. It took her all of fifteen seconds. What felt like another ten seconds she spent locking the dog collar around my neck and attaching the leash. Just how good was she at this, anyway?

I had propped myself up on my elbows during our saucy little exchange, and now Erica grabbed the metal ring at the top of the head harness and pushed me down flat onto the bed, curling the chain leash in her hand and holding my face absolutely still. My mouth spread wide around the ball gag, and just as an experiment, I tried to talk.

"Slaves are meant to be seen and not heard," said Erica. "Except when I slap you. Then you can whimper."

"Yes, Mistress," I tried to say, but it came out as a strangled yelp, which only seemed to turn her on more. She grabbed the leather restraints and quickly cinched them around my wrists, expertly threading the nylon webbing through the headboard. Then she climbed off the bed and gave my ankles the same treatment. The rough way she grabbed my legs to position them just so made my cock surge against my belly.

Erica circled the bed once like a beast surveying her domain, a cruel little smile on her face. She hooked her thumbs in her little black lace thong and pulled it down her thighs, revealing a freshly-shaved pussy, yet another something I wasn't expecting. Stepping out of her thong, she pushed it into my face, smearing the crotch—soaked with her juices even though she'd barely worn the thong at all—over my face. I took a deep breath of her scent and felt my cock respond with a fresh pulse of excitement.

Then Erica descended on me hungrily, pouncing on the bed, one hand grabbing the ring of the head harness and the other curving around my hard cock.

"My slave knows what his mistress wants," she growled. "Stay hard long enough and maybe I'll let you eat me out." She threw one lithe leg over my hip and stretched on top of me, guiding my cock between her spread legs. Her cunt was molten, slicker and wetter than I'd ever felt it, as she sank down on my cock. A shudder went through me as she pushed herself onto me and sat up, towering over me and looking absolutely delectable as she began to grind slowly back and forth.

She reached down and dug her nails into my bare chest; my back arched as she left long, angry furrows. My hips lifted off the bed and drove my cock deeper into her; she pushed down against me and wriggled back and forth, stroking the head of my cock against her G-spot. She lay down on top of me, pumping her hips up and down. She seized the ring of my head harness with one hand, wrapped my leash around her other and growled into my ear.

"You like that, slave? You like servicing your mistress with that big, hard cock?"

I nodded fervently, feeling the pressure against my head as she held me still both at the top of my head and at my collar. Her eyes closed as she began to moan.

"Right…there…," she sighed. "Don't move, slave. Hold absolutely still."

She began to fuck me hungrily, and I had to fight to obey her command. I wanted to fuck her hard, but I didn't dare— even after weeks of relatively vanilla sex, I knew from experience that Erica came faster when she could do the fucking. I struggled to hold still as she pumped her cunt down onto my cock, her moans growing in volume as she got closer. I also had to fight not to come—I didn't want to give up my hard cock just yet. I wanted to please her, and I knew my mistress would come several times before she was satisfied.

"Right...fucking...there...," she groaned, and came, her body shuddering against mine as she drove herself down onto my cock. I could feel her pussy clenching around my shaft as her orgasm overtook her. She only stopped for a moment, though, as the shivers of her completion went through her. Then she was at it again, fucking me harder than ever and sitting bolt upright, her yoga-trained thighs lifting her wholly off of my cock and then ramming her down hard onto me again.

I wanted to tell her I was going to come, that I couldn't hold off any longer—but all I could do was whimper deep inside the gag. I was an instant away from letting go when Erica shuddered again and, still gripping the leash, drew her nails down my chest once more, this time breaking the skin. The pain brought me back into my body and away from my orgasm as she came for the second time. I held myself still, desperately trying not to come as I looked up at her and felt my arousal throbbing powerfully through my whole body.

"That's a good cock slave," she told me. "You've earned your reward."

Her thighs shaking a little, Erica drew herself off of me and quickly unbuckled the harness that held the ball gag in my mouth. I took a deep breath as she pulled the ball free and forced the harness up over my forehead. She passed the leash into her other hand and turned around on top of me, spreading her legs and settling her pussy down onto my face.

"Show your mistress how much you appreciate her using your cock," she snarled, her voice sounding more forceful than ever. My tongue settled onto her clit and began to seethe against it; she rode my face upright as she ground her hips back and forth. "Taste your fucking cock," she growled, and her voice descended into whimpers as I serviced her pussy, licking all the way from her entrance to her clit and back again, then suckling gently on her clit. I *could* taste an unfamiliar musk mixed with that of her pussy. She reached down and grabbed my cock around the base, behind my balls, and squeezed—just firmly enough to make me squirm.

"Harder," she ordered. "Suck my clit harder and I'll let you come when I do."

She began to stroke my cock as I obeyed; she knew I was as close as she was. As I worked her clit faster, she slumped forward onto me, tugging on the leash even as she guided my cock between her lips. She began to suck me fiercely, matching every stroke of my tongue on her clit. My hips rose to meet her, and I knew I was going to come in her mouth.

I exploded moments before Erica did; her lips clamped tight halfway down my shaft and she took every drop of my come. My cock muffled the cries of her third orgasm, but I could still hear them and, even more so, feel the vibrations of them coursing through my body. As she finished coming, she lifted herself off of my face and then pushed down again, the momentary break intensifying her orgasm. She sucked my cock dry as I increased pressure on her clit, and when she finished swallowing everything she slid off of me, turned around, and lay fully atop my body. She pressed her lips to mine and the unexpected taste of my own come did nothing but make me descend further into my role as her slave. Her sticky tongue slid into my mouth and I opened wide for it, my cock still spasming from my intense orgasm.

Finally spent, my mistress lay on top of me and gently

rattled my chain. When she finally reached up and unclipped the webbing that held my wrists to the bed, I put my arms around her and held her close.

"So, slave," she sighed. "Were you surprised?"

"Oh yes," I said sheepishly. "It's exactly what I deserved."

She gripped my leash and smiled.

"You've got that right, slave. That'll teach you to peek."

My face reddened and my mistress nuzzled her face against my ear.

"So I was right," she said. "You did peek. You're a naughty little slave, you know."

"Oh yes," I said. "I most certainly am."

O Naughty Night
Simone Harlow

On the ninth day of Christmas my true love gave to me: one round-trip ticket for the hell out of here. Actually, Liz Phair blasted on my headphones, not that stupid Xmas ditty. Now *that* caught the feeling I was having as I rode the elevator up to my seventh-floor office. I flat out refused to listen to the canned Christmas blah blah blah playing on the elevator's speaker. The music reminded me of Chinese water torture. Frankly, there was nothing that was going to cheer me up except escape.

Christmas was bad enough as it is, but who could get their serious ho ho ho on in the middle of a Las Vegas heat wave? I'm a Denver girl, born and bred. Christmas ain't Christmas unless you're facing a case of frostbite on the way out the front door to pick up the morning newspaper.

For the five thousandth time in the last fifteen minutes I

considered a Buddhist conversion. Not that it would happen. The firm of Benton, Graves and Campbell, would have a collective stroke if anyone so much as slipped his left pinkie toe over the line of conventional. And since they paid me a lot of money to be normal, I did a great job of appearing so. I coulda been an actress. BG&C may be located in the heart of Sin City, but these guys put the *up* in *upstanding*. Call me a conformist, but I so love to feed my shoe addiction. So I played their game.

Balancing the eggnog latte with my briefcase, purse, *and* gym bag, I struggled to open the door to my office. I hate when I leave my third hand at home. Ian Tapping, the techno wunderkind, strolled over and helped me. Of course, no words were spoken, not a hey, hidey ho, or kiss my ass passed through those perfectly chiseled lips. He was, without a doubt, the epitome of the strong silent type.

"Thanks," I mumbled.

He just kinda grunted, "No problem, Callie," and went on his merry way.

I shuffled through the door and dropped everything on the floor. Everything but the coffee. That truly would have been tragic. Checking my watch, I saw that I had ten minutes before all hell broke loose. I decided to leave the bags where they fell and sit down, put my feet up on my desk and enjoy my coffee. I had earned the right.

On my chair, I found a present. Red metallic paper covered a shallow square box. A perfectly tied gold ribbon formed a big loopy bow. Normally, I hate surprises, but I do so adore presents. And I could spot expensive wrapping paper in a Denver snow at five hundred paces. High-priced wrapping paper usually means a high-end gift. Of course, I picked the box up and shook it.

Very lightweight, I thought, *and no telltale rattle. That means it's probably not jewelry*. I could live with that. I put down the coffee, because this needed the two-handed treatment. Slipping my finger under the taped edge, I contemplated: Slow or fast? Neat or messy? Oh, fuck it, I wanted what was in the box. I ripped the paper, tossed the shredded mess aside, and flipped open the lid. A gold foil note card rested on the white tissue paper. Dare I read?

Well hell yeah.

On the first day of Christmas… Those ellipses get me every time.

More and more curious, I dug at the packing and was greeted with a vision of black lace nestled in very innocent white tissue paper.

My heart started racing.

Carefully, I slipped my forefinger under the delicate G-string. As I rubbed the soft material between my finger and thumb, a shiver ran down my spine. Silk. My fav. The tiny elastic band caressed my skin. For a second, the material was cool, but it heated quickly. Oh, this was nice. Very, very nice.

The sheer lacy front panel was shaped like a butterfly. Two rhinestones dotted the tips of each wing. I lifted the thong to my face and rubbed the material on my cheek. Intricately woven French lace. I closed my eyes, enjoying the sensation. If I wanted to wear this, I was going to have to go Brazilian. Just the thought of going totally bare sent decadent chills to my pussy. I'd always wanted to, but never had the nerve.

Now who'd given me such a tasty little present? Someone who knew I had a secret yen for things naughty? Who could it be? It appeared I had a Secret Santa.

A knock broke my concentration.

I shoved the box aside with my free hand and hid the panties behind my back just as the door opened. All I needed was to be caught feeling up some undies while on the clock. How did one explain that to one's boss?

Ian stood in my doorway staring at me.

"Yes?"

"Callie, do you think you can make it to the meeting anytime in the next hour?"

Jerk-off, I thought. Okay, *sexy* jerk-off in a geeky, hunky sort of way. Getting nasty with him had been a goal of mine for a while now. "No problem, I'll be right there."

He stepped into the office. "What are you hiding?"

I batted my eyelashes at him hoping I looked innocent. "Nothing."

He grunted and left the office.

That was a close one.

The next morning, as I rode up in the elevator, the silk thong rubbed against my clit. God, I felt naughty. I was so energized I hadn't even made my morning pilgrimage to Starbucks, and I was so wet I thought I was going to slide right off the elevator and into my office. The Christmas music didn't even bother me. With my silk and lace panties, I could conquer the world.

Somehow I found myself whistling "Have Yourself a Merry Little Christmas" as I opened the door to my office. And what awaited my wondering eyes, but a pristine wrapped package of green and gold. O Merry Christmas to little old *moi*.

I dumped my briefcase, purse, and gym bag on the floor and ran to my desk. I shredded the paper in seconds and opened the box. There was the card.

On the second day of Christmas…

A pair of black opera gloves lay nestled in the white tissue paper. Damn, if I couldn't wait until tomorrow.

On the third day my secret admirer gave to me a pair of black patent leather platform stiletto Mary Janes. The shoes were sublime. Every one of my whipped-cream, nasty Catholic girl fantasies featured shoes like this. As my palms began to sweat, the logical accountant Callie reared her analytical head.

Who knew that I dreamed about submission in my darkest dreams? The only place I dared to let my imagination run wild was online. I never used my company account, just my personal laptop. I rarely brought it to work. As the only woman at BG&C in management, I played hardball with the big boys in their sandbox. I didn't let them inside my head.

Strangely, I was more turned on than scared.

As I cradled one of the shoes between my breasts, my nipples hardened to almost painful points. The earthy smell of fine grain leather was intoxicating. Whoever wanted to romp nasty with me had the money to afford expensive recreational trinkets. My kind of playmate. The mystery thickened.

The next morning, the elevator was having bad mojo so I ran up the stairs. I was so excited to get to work I'd skipped the gym, but I was covered after seven flights.

When I reached my office, I was a bit surprised *not* to find a box. Disappointment engulfed me, but I didn't have long to pout. As if on cue, my secretary buzzed informing me that the partners needed to see me.

After an hour of doing my I'm-a-good-and-loyal-worker-bee routine, I returned to my office to instantly uplifted spirits. Wrapped in silver paper was my present. My faith in the world restored, I ripped the paper to find my card and a pair of sheer black thigh-high stockings. I had to control myself and not slip them on until I got home.

The weekend came and went in blur. I spent most of Saturday and Sunday parading around my house in my new ensemble. I have to say, I felt pretty damned sexy. My poor little vibrator got one hell of a workout. I'm sure my battery operated boyfriend—or BOB as I like to call him—was happy to see Monday morning so he could get a much-needed rest.

I couldn't wait either. In fact, Monday couldn't arrive fast enough. I hurried into my office and spotted my new surprise on the cherry credenza. I clapped my hands, then closed the door and flipped the lock. Sometimes a girl just needs to be alone. I opened the box to discover a black mask with ruffled edges. *Ooh la la.*

The next day, a sterling silver dog collar arrived. The best treat of all was that I wore it that day and everyone commented on the beautiful necklace. Of course, I wanted my very special someone to know I loved my new present.

How much further would this go? As much as the anticipation to find out who was behind all this was killing me, I almost didn't want it to end. Each day my Secret Santa seemed to top himself.

Then it was three days before we closed the office for Christmas break and I was wondering what was in store for me now. In my office I received my answer. A black bralett was my next gift. The open cups would frame my breasts perfectly. After I stripped off my shirt, I replaced my old bra with the new one. I felt absolutely decadent with my nipples surrounded by sheer black material. I didn't want to take it off. Of course, it would mean wearing my jacket all day, but a day in Vegas without air-conditioning was a day in hell.

Two more days until Christmas. The elevator cranked to

my floor. What would my next gift be? And more importantly, who was dressing me and why? There had to be an end to my story, but I couldn't even begin to guess.

Inside my office, I spotted the red-papered box. This box was different, nearly two feet long and rectangular. I couldn't imagine what was inside. My lack of patience got the best of me and I ripped the paper to reveal a heavy wooden box. Carved into the dark wood was an image of a horse and rider taking a fence. I flicked up the brass tab and lifted the lid. My mouth dropped open. Resting inside the red velvet lining was a riding crop. A lump formed in my throat. I had never seen something so beautiful. It had a braided leather grip with a black leather tassel. I became instantly wet as I stroked my fingers along the grip. My pussy just sort of clinched up. A smart girl would have brought her vibe to work, locked the door and had a field day. Guess this wasn't my day to be the smart girl.

The door crashed open and good old Ian stuck his head in. "Where's my monthly projections?"

I was still so dazed from the gift that his words barely penetrated my brain. "What?"

He stepped into the office and slammed the door. "What's in the box?"

Think quick, Callie! I whacked the lid close. "My dad's Christmas present."

"Really?"

"The projections are being copied as we speak," I managed to stammer, desperate to change the subject.

"Nice box."

"This old thing?" My heart raced.

He took another step into my office. "Can I have a look?"

I tried to hide it behind my back. "I'd prefer you didn't...." God that sounded so rude.

He smiled. "No problem." He backed out of my office and closed the door.

For the first time since he'd started working for the company he'd actually smiled. This was a *true* Christmas miracle.

After he left I noticed there was no card. Disappointed, I closed the box. But when I returned from lunch, there on my desk was a familiar gold foil envelope. I slipped my finger under the flap.

On the last day of Christmas my true love met me after the Christmas party dressed to play.

Sipping a glass of punch at the party, I was a little nervous; more so than I had anticipated. As fascinating as an uncontrolled sexual encounter might be in my fantasy, I liked being in control of my life. I should have just taken my riding crop and sexy underwear and gone home to my cat where it was safe. Besides, I had to pack and catch a plane for my family's version of sleigh bells and snow. Glancing at the clock in the main lobby, I tried to decide whether I wanted to play or go home.

Decisions, decisions.

More time passed and the partiers had thinned out, but I wasn't any closer to an answer. Should I stay or should I go? How many times do you get to live out a secret dream? Not many in my case, since I've been busy climbing the ladder of success. What did I really have to lose? That answered my question. There were six men left: Ian, Mike from sales, and Bill from accounting were the ones I knew fairly well. The others included the president of company, Mr. Old and Wrinkly. *Please don't let it be him,* I prayed. Don't get me wrong, older men can turn my switch. The right ones. If

Harrison Ford jumped into my game, I'd drop trou and call him Daddy all day long. But Indiana wasn't here and I was stuck with Old Prune Juice. And that was not going to happen in this lifetime.

The other two men I knew by sight. If I had my wish, I decided, it would either be Ian or Mike. Ian because he had been my secret fantasy since his first day on the job, and Mike because he's got a body that would make Vin Diesel jealous. I checked my watch. Time to make a move. Without another thought, I made a beeline for my office.

After I had undressed, I took all my presents out and lovingly put on each item except the crop. In a strange way, I went into a trance. I was buzzing with excitement, my heart was racing, my pussy wet.

The chime of my clock hit eight just as I pulled the mask over my eyes and sat in my desk chair. "Merry Christmas, Callie."

It was Ian. "How did you know?" I whispered. "I mean, how'd you know all my fantasies?"

He sighed. "I serviced your laptop."

"You snooped."

I heard him chuckle. "Show me the riding crop."

Wishing I could see his face, I lifted the crop and held it out.

He took it from me. "Stand up."

Good little girl that I am, I did exactly as I was told.

Ian took my arm and walked me slowly around the edge of my desk.

"Bend over," he whispered near my ear.

Well, of course I did. Quickly, he slid my G-string down my thighs. Then he softly began caressing my ass. His fingers felt light and soothing as they ran up my skin. Who would ever have pegged Ian the techno god as a freak? This was the best present ever.

Without warning, the tip of the crop hit my ass. I sank my teeth into my bottom lip to stop from crying out. Pain radiated up my backside, but I also felt the stirring of pleasure. Again the crop hit me, and I gasped. Heat danced over my naked skin. God, I was wet.

Bracing myself for the next blow, I was surprised when I felt him palm my buttcheek.

"I have been wanting your ass from day one."

My ass as well as my pussy clinched up. Another decadent shiver crept up my entire body. "It's all yours tonight."

One of his fingers slipped between my cheeks. I wanted to relax and let this happen, but I was too anxious to get things started. *Hurry, hurry*, I begged silently as I stuck my bottom up higher, giving his naughty finger all the ass it could possibly want.

A series of sharp quick blows rained down on my butt. Hard enough to make me forget about his finger still working its way up and down my ass slit. I shook with anticipation.

Ian slipped his finger inside my pussy and flicked my clit. My knees buckled, but I quickly recovered. I sunk my teeth even harder into my bottom lip to stop from screaming. A picture of the office staff bolting into my office to find me with my ass in the air and Ian fingering me flashed in my head. I pushed the thought away so I didn't ruin my good time. Good old Ian commanded that finger like a pro. I kept pushing my hips back trying to get everything I could.

"Stay still," he instructed.

"Sorry." I stopped wiggling. "Is this what you want?"

"Good girl."

He flicked the crop once again across my bare cheeks as

he worked his finger inside of me. This man had talent. My pussy was soaked. My arms buckled under me as Ian continued to flog me. My bare breast touched the hard wood surface of my desk. My nipples were so hard they almost hurt. My butt was on fire, but I still wanted more. Squeezing my eyes shut, I tried to stop the waves of sensation overtaking me. Spasms of pleasure began deep in my pussy, and I knew I was going to come. One more swat of the crop and I just let go. My whole body shook with the force of my orgasm.

Landing flush on top of my desk, I tried to catch my breath. I had just gotten the best holly jolly of my life.

"Merry Christmas, Callie," Ian whispered as he took off my mask.

Christmas Morning
N. T. Morley

Before she had quite woken up on Christmas morning, Christelle felt that she was alone in the bed. When she opened her eyes and saw the indentation that her lover had left, she rolled over onto his side of the mattress, feeling his lingering warmth and deeply inhaling his scent. She had forgotten that it was Christmas until after she had realized that she was horny. As thoughts filtered through her mind, she felt the pressure of her stiffening nipples against the sheets, felt the familiar pulse between her legs, a heat and hunger that always came when she wanted sex. She wished Aaron was here against her, climbing on top of her, or perhaps guiding her down under the covers to take his cock in her mouth. She ran her fingers lazily up her thighs and touched her smooth pussy, feeling how wet it was. She rubbed her clit lightly and gasped at the sensation, moaning softly. If Aaron were here, he would fuck her. She wondered where he'd gotten to.

He had been away for more than three weeks, traveling on business while she attended to her own career. In fact, she'd been so busy she'd hardly had any time to think about what she was going to get him. When Aaron had returned home late last night, Christmas Eve, Christelle had been excited to see him and deeply horny from weeks of deprivation. But Aaron had been too tired from his long plane trip to make love, and the two of them had tumbled swiftly into bed and soon were asleep. She could still feel the ache of pent-up desire for her absent lover. She rubbed herself and moaned, very close to coming—but not wanting to get off without him.

When Christelle finally slipped out of the tangled covers and put on her robe, her legs felt weak and her nipples rubbed firmly against the rough terry cloth. She found Aaron sitting on the living room sofa by the Christmas tree, drinking coffee and reading the newspaper. A series of packages wrapped in silver, gold, red, and green had been neatly arrayed in front of the tree. Aaron wore his silk robe, which hung open far enough to show Christelle her lover's lightly furred chest. She went up to him, sat in his broad lap, and cuddled up against that chest, running her fingers over it as she kissed his neck.

"Merry Christmas," he told her. "Ready to open your presents?"

"They're for me?" she asked, feigning innocence. "But I didn't get you anything!"

"Then you'd better open *your* presents, or it'll hardly be Christmas, will it?"

"Promise you're not mad that I didn't get you anything?" she asked.

Aaron smiled. "Open your presents," he said warmly.

Christelle retrieved the boxes, counting five. She set them next to Aaron on the sofa and sat on his lap again. She loved the fact that Aaron was big enough to sit on. She picked up the smallest box and shook it. She heard the faint rustling of metal—it sounded almost like a chain. A necklace? Unable to stand the suspense, she ripped open the wrapping and took off the top of the glittering gold box. Her mouth dropped open.

"I hope you're not wearing anything under that robe," said Aaron, tugging away the terry cloth as he took the nipple clamps out of the box. He exposed Christelle's nipples and she moaned softly as he fitted the clamps over them. She gasped as the faint throb of pain settled into her. She felt her clit swell to match the sensation in her nipples, and her pussy suddenly felt hot and tight.

"Next present," said Aaron.

Breathing heavily, Christelle picked up the next smallest box and tore off the wrapping. When the box top came off, she stared, wide-eyed, hand at her mouth.

"Here," said Aaron. "Let me put it on for you."

Christelle obediently sat still in Aaron's lap as his big hands drew the thick black leather collar around her throat, buckled it, and clicked the padlock closed. She felt the pressure of the nipple clamps increasing as her nipples hardened still more. Her pussy was beginning to hurt, it felt so swollen and hungry.

"Open the next box, dear," said Aaron.

Christelle obeyed, quickly tearing the silver wrapping and opening the box. She tried to suppress the moan that issued from her lips as she looked inside.

"Be a good girl," said Aaron. "Stand up and take off your robe."

Christelle stood and slid her terry-cloth robe over her shoulders. It fell in a pool on the floor. She leaned forward, closing her eyes. Aaron had to remove one nipple clamp to thread the chain that connected them through the twin openings of the PVC bra. When he told her to turn around, she obeyed, and he fastened the strap tight across her back, making her nipples stand out distended through the tight, tiny openings. He replaced the nipple clamps and nodded toward the next package.

Christelle curled up in Aaron's lap, nude except for the collar, bra, and nipple clamps. The next box was considerably larger. She plucked off the ribbon, tore the gold paper and opened it.

Her heart pounded so hard she could hear it in her ears.

"Bend over," said Aaron.

Christelle could feel herself shaking as she stood up and bent over the coffee table, supporting herself with her outstretched arms. Aaron fitted the enormous dildo into the harness. Christelle was wet to the point of dripping. But this dildo was considerably bigger than any she'd ever taken, bigger even than Aaron's cock. He teased open Christelle's pussy lips and inserted the dildo with a single rough thrust that made her gasp and straighten up.

"I told you to bend over," he growled.

Christelle obediently bent back over, lifting her ass high in the air as Aaron pushed the dildo all the way into her and buckled the harness around her waist and thighs. The harness was fitted with a rubber ridge that pressed very hard against her clit as Aaron cinched the buckles tight. Aaron licked his thumb, and then as he pried her smooth rear cheeks apart, Christelle felt the firmness of pressure circling her exposed anus.

"I had to look everywhere to find one that kept your asshole exposed," said Aaron. "I prefer to keep it exposed whenever possible."

Christelle responded with an inarticulate moan, her body swaying with the sensations of her stuffed-full pussy.

"Next package," said Aaron.

Christelle was frightened and excited at what she might find. She sat in Aaron's lap with great difficulty, every movement of her lower body seeming to press the dildo deeper inside her and make her shiver with sensation. She was very close to a climax, but it wouldn't do to come until she'd opened the last present.

She tore the red and green paper and opened the box.

"You know what to do, darling," smiled Aaron.

And Christelle did. Her hands were shaking, she was so turned on. She took out the big bottle of lube and pulled open Aaron's robe, revealing his fully erect cock. She went down on her knees and took it in her mouth, licking up the shaft to the head. Then Christelle drizzled some lube over the head and smeared it down the shaft. Turning around, Christelle held Aaron's cock in one hand and guided it smoothly between her rear cheeks. Aaron took firm hold of Christelle's hips and pulled her down onto him. Her eyes went wide as she was forced down onto Aaron's cock. She could feel the thickness of his shaft pressing deep into her body, rubbing against the fullness of the dildo already penetrating her. Aaron got a good hold of her and wriggled her down more fully onto his cock, until he was thrust as far as he could go into her tight back door.

Christelle was going to come.

Aaron bent her forward very far so he could increase the friction as he guided her up and down on his cock. His eyes narrowed. He pushed Christelle forward so far that she had to steady herself with her hands on the coffee table. Only the head of his cock now remained in her ass, the shaft glistening with lubricant. Aaron tugged down the edge of the harness and looked at the name tattooed at the base of Christelle's spine, at the very top of her rear furrow.

"See, darling? I lied," she whimpered. "I did get you a present."

"It's lovely," he said. "The best I could have hoped for."

Then he took firm hold of Christelle's hips and pulled her onto his cock again, the single thrust taking her down to the very base. Christelle gasped. The quick insertion drove her over the edge, and she came as Aaron began to force her up and down on his cock. Her orgasm intensified as she tightened her thighs and pounded herself up and down on him, making the silver chain of the nipple clamps sway back and forth against her chest. The orgasm was unexpected in its intensity, and Christelle was still coming when Aaron groaned and let go inside her a moment later, filling her rear entrance with his come.

She relaxed against him, leaning back as his hands came up to pluck the clamps from her breasts. The sudden rush of sensation made her whimper in mingled pain and pleasure. "Did you like your present?" she asked.

He rolled her onto her belly across his knee. Tugging the strap of the harness down again, he ran his finger over the cursive letters of his name.

"It's a very merry Christmas," he said, and pulled her back onto him.

Here Comes Santa Claus
Thomas S. Roche

It took Emma until Richmond Station to stop fuming. Why did she always forget about how much Christmas pissed her off? The required shopping for holiday gifts irritated her, but the real ballbusting started when she showed up at her parents' place for Christmas. If it hadn't been the repeated quizzing from her grandmother about when and whether she planned to get married (she was a sophomore in fucking college, for Christ's sake), it would have been the comment by her mother about how women who expected to go anywhere in life really shouldn't tart themselves up like punk rock sluts.

This year it was the nose ring. Last year it had been the bleach-blonde hair. Emma felt particularly foolish, because she'd dyed her hair chestnut-brown just a week ago in anticipation of the Christmas holidays. She thought Mom had gotten

over the nose ring—but in fact she seemed to have been saving it to comment on at a really inopportune time.

In any event, if Emma hadn't been so annoyed already,
her lecherous Uncle Fred's dirty jokes and Aunt Tiffy's pre-
dictable tendency to drink herself into a celebratory stupor,
punctuated by the reliving of family trauma from 1965,
would have really pissed her off. Luckily, Emma herself had
slung back a few Jack and ginger's, so by the time the two
sisters began arguing about the disposition of their beloved
convertible Cadillac (circa 1958) she was happily in the arms
of Morpheus, freezing to death on the chaise lounge out on
the back porch. Luckily the sun had come out and Emma
had narrowly avoided frostbite, awakening just in time for a
drunken exchange of unwished-for presents.

When she transferred off Amtrak, Emma decided not to
go straight back to the dorms; it was Saturday, and almost
no one would be home from Christmas break just yet. She
didn't particularly want to socialize, but she didn't want to be
alone, either. She decided she had an errand to run.

She'd taken the noon train—the earliest she could get any
of her crazy relatives to drive her to the station. When she
got off the local train and trudged up the street past shivering homeless folks, she was seized with middle-class guilt and
started distributing her quarters. By the time she arrived at
the sex toy store, she was on the edge of desperation.

The place was deserted. It was the Saturday after Christmas, and no one was thinking about sex, apparently. Except
her.

The shop was staffed entirely by women who made the
pierced and plaid-skirted Emma look like a member of the
Republican National Committee. Three clerks—one young
butch dyke, one purple-haired goth-looking chick, and a

dark-skinned transwoman in improbable heels—were lean-ing against the counter looking bored.

"Hi," said the babydyke. "Can I help you find some-thing?"

"I need the dirtiest sex toy you have," Emma blurted, dropping her army-green duffel bag near the door.

"Um," said the babydyke. "We, um, ah…dirty?"

Emma tried to clarify and got pretty much nowhere. "I don't mean *dirty* dirty. I mean…I don't know what I mean. Something really bad. I mean badass, not low quality. About a hundred dollars?"

"Christmas money," said the transwoman.

"You know it," said Emma.

All three employees nodded knowingly.

"Rough time with the parents?"

Emma slumped into the armchair next to the counter and looked up miserably.

"You want to buy something to take care of yourself."

"Yeah, I guess that's a more positive way to put it," said Emma. "Something filthy."

Several moments of silence passed before the butch dyke piped up with a smile: "Filthy is all in the mind."

"Oh, I know," said Emma. "But right now, my mind says 'filthy, filthy, filthy.'"

"All right, then," said the goth chick helpfully. "What does filthy, um, mean to you?"

Emma's eyes flickered over the racks and racks of multi-colored dildos, settling on one that was particularly garish in its size and realism. Fitted with a suction cup, the thing was networked with bulging veins and an improbably thick head. It must have been twelve inches long.

Emma felt her body begin to react before she realized it.

The flush went right to her cheeks and she felt her nipples hardening inside the tight sweater she wore.

"Maybe I just need a really, really big dick," said Emma, as if thinking to herself.

She crossed her arms and legs nervously, smiling as innocently as she could manage.

The transwoman came around from behind the counter. "Ah, yes," she said. "A common sentiment. But make sure your eyes aren't bigger than your…appetite. Would you like to see some more samples?"

Emma awkwardly followed the transwoman around the store, viewing several walls' worth of phallic toys and hearing a lecture about the relative merits of silicone versus jelly rubber. She tried very hard to listen politely and not keep looking back at the thick-headed cock with its beckoning veins and stiff shaft.

When the tour was finished, Emma cleared her throat and said, "I, um, I think I'll take that one. The, uh, the big one."

"Excellent choice," said the transwoman with a knowing smile.

"I'll get one from the back," said the butch dyke.

"And of course don't forget the lube," called the goth woman helpfully from across the room.

"I was getting to that, Janessa," said the transwoman, flourishing her hand Vanna-style over the impressive wall of lube bottles. Since the dildo Emma wanted was well under a hundred dollars, she spent the rest of her Christmas money on numerous bottles of lube and a glossy fetish magazine of pinup models being spanked. What could she say? It caught her eye.

The total came to $101.53. Emma fished around for dimes and pennies and gave the transwoman exact change.

"And since you've topped a hundred dollars," said the transwoman as she put the toy, lubes, and magazine into a bag, "You get one of our seasonal gifts." She produced a Santa hat with the logo of the store—a woman pleasuring herself.

"Now that," said Emma, "is filthy."

"I thought you'd like it," said the transwoman with a wink. "Come again!"

Emma thanked the three women and left the store, feeling a rather uncomfortable heat growing inside her as she noted the daunting weight of the toy in her bag.

The dorms were deserted, as Emma had figured they would be. It was just as well, because she'd spent the whole bus ride thinking about what she was going to do when she got back to her dorm room. There weren't many PG-rated thoughts left in her head.

Emma felt sweaty from the overheated bus and the many layers of winter clothes piled on her. But she couldn't bear the thought of running down the hall to the shared bathroom to shower. Instead, she upended the plain brown bag over her bed, which she'd irresponsibly left unmade when she'd departed for the holiday. The dildo looked an awful lot bigger and more thickly-veined in this light, even with no smaller, smoother dildos to compare it to.

Just handling the big dildo—unrolling a condom over its massive length—turned Emma on. She felt incredibly naughty knowing she'd spent her Christmas money from her conservative relatives on what was presumably the biggest dick she would ever put anywhere near her pussy.

Emma stripped off her clothes and began to rub her clit. She opened up the fetish magazine and leafed one-handed through page after page of fetching retro-clad pinup girls bent over men's and women's knees. She felt her pleasure mounting as she rubbed her clit faster. Then she turned the page and saw something that sent a surge of excitement through her.

It was a picture of a woman in a latex elf costume, bent over Santa's knee. Her tight-fitting green latex dress was pulled up to her waist and Santa's hand was connecting with her full, rounded lace-clad buttocks, squarely between her emerald green garters.

"Oh, that's filthy," said Emma out loud, and remembered the hat.

She put on the Santa hat and grabbed her hand mirror from the nightstand. She looked at herself in the hat, admiring the way the woman pleasuring herself reflected her own frantic rubbing of her clit. Approaching her orgasm quickly as she looked from the mirror to the naughty elf and back again, Emma tossed the mirror on her pillow and reached for the dildo.

"Make it real, Santa," she said, indulging her private sense of humor. Surprising herself, she found that talking dirty about Santa actually did something for her. "Make it fucking real, Santa. Spank my fucking naughty elf bottom."

Eyeing the magazine, she rubbed her clit with one hand and guided the thick head of the dildo up to her pussy.

She realized with the first pressure against her cunt that there was no fucking way this thing was going anywhere. She grabbed a lube bottle at random and drizzled lube over her pussy and over the latex-sheathed head of the dildo.

"Make it fucking real, Santa," she said. "Shove that big thing in my pussy."

The pressure against her entrance made her moan. God, this thing was fucking huge. Her pussy lips curved around the thickness of the head, but even with a firm pressure the big thing failed utterly to enter her. Emma rubbed her clit further and began to press the cockhead rhythmically against her opening.

"Make it fucking real, Santa," she moaned. "Oh, Santa, you've got the biggest dick in the world. Shove it in me. Shove your fucking cock in me—oh!"

Emma came, her whole body shivering with pleasure as the pressure at the entrance to her cunt brought her off. She kept rubbing her clit rapidly as her orgasm heightened, and her glazed eyes roved over the naughty elf in Santa's lap as she whimpered, "Fuck me, Santa, fuck me!"

The last spasms of Emma's orgasm exploded through her and her back arched as she pressed herself against the bed. She grabbed the dildo with both hands and forced it rhythmically against her pussy, gasping, "Yes, Santa, yes!" as she came. Finally the tension went out of her body and she lay there, holding the dildo between her legs.

When she looked down at it, she was struck once more by just how big it was. How had she ever thought she was going to put that thing inside her?

But she could still feel the warmth of her orgasm inside her. She smiled and peeled the condom off the dildo, tossing it into the bedside garbage can. Curling up on her bed, Emma tucked the dildo and magazine under her pillow and put the lube in her nightstand. Exhausted from her long journey and session of self-pleasuring, she decided it was time for a nap.

As she slipped into a welcomed alpha state, she kept her hand curved around Santa's dick, reminding herself that it had, for all practical purposes, been purchased for her by her arch-conservative relatives.

Out on the quad, Emma could hear someone singing Christmas carols. She even found herself humming along with "Here Comes Santa Claus." As she drifted to sleep, she wondered if anyone else was getting off on the tune.

What I Really Want for Christmas
Lynne Jamneck

"You're working on Christmas Eve?!"

Jools looked at me incredulously. A skinny waiter arrived with our coffee and croissants. Outside the coffee bar, Cape Town's pedestrian traffic was picking up. I thought of a valid excuse.

"Well, not yet," I finally said. "But I will be. What else should I be doing?"

Jools made a sour face, scrunching the freckles on her nose together, and stirred sugar into her cup. She gave me an even more ridiculous look when I shook a packet of artificial sweetener in my own coffee.

"What?" I asked when I noticed how she stared at me from above the rim of her cup.

"When was the last time you got laid?"

I almost choked on the piping hot coffee. "Excuse me?"

"You heard me. Christ—sweetener in your coffee? Next thing you're going to tell me is you've committed to a vow of celibacy. I shudder to think."

"Well," I smiled sarcastically, "I could do without all the women-bullshit for a while, actually."

Jools waved a finger at me. "Did I not warn you about that chick? What was her name—Tanya something-or-other? Never trust a woman whose name begins with a *T*. They're all fuckin' crazy."

"Jools, there was nothing wrong with Tanya."

"Oh? I asked her once if she knew Vita Sackville-West. She asked me if that was the latest designer line from Milan."

I laughed. "Okay, so she was a little shallow."

"Pfff—shallow? She couldn't fill up an espresso cup."

"Maybe. But she was hell on wheels in bed."

"God. You're getting that far-off look in your eyes again. That's it," Jools stated. "You're spending Christmas with me on the farm."

I shook my head vigorously. "Whoa, hold up. Your folks? *That* farm? Those people are insane. Last time I was there over the holidays they all wore those pointy hats with the bells at the top. Chanel, no less. Every time someone would get up to fetch something from the kitchen it started to ring some robotic Christmas carol. Fucking drove me insane. No way. No go."

Jools waited patiently across the table. "Are you quite finished?"

"Yes. And my case well stated, I think."

"We were fifteen then. Everything irritated and drove us insane. Besides, my parents are having a Christmas weekend for underprivileged kids this year. They're finally moving out of their Rich and Shallow phase into their Rich and Feeling Guilty phase. Come on—there's even going to be a real Santa Claus."

"What the hell am I, six years old? Besides, an old guy—probably alcoholic—dressed up in a red suit is hardly my idea of fun."

"Nor is it mine, Kat. At least we won't be the center of attention. Plus, we can get horribly drunk on my father's spiked eggnog. Then we can sit around and try to figure out how many of the straight people my parents invited for their big dinner have had affairs with one another."

"That is fun, isn't it?"

Jools winked. "Come on; still want to be working for that hard-ass boss of yours when you should be out there in the Styx having fun with me?"

The conspiratorial gleam in her eyes was more than I could handle. Always has been.

"Somehow I think you've just persuaded me."

She shrugged casually. "I'm convincing that way."

Jools had an ancient Ford pickup, which we drove all the way up to her parents' farm in Uniondale. The area was famous for the legend about a woman who had been killed in a car accident while she was driving in the area with her fiancé. Apparently she still haunted the road at night, thumbing rides from unsuspecting motorists.

As we neared the main gate of Dover Stud Farm (or as Jools liked to refer to it, Studly-Do-Right), Jools asked: "You remember Annie Small? She used to be my father's farrier. Shoed his horses."

"Annie Sparks!" I slapped my knee and made Jools laugh. "Jesus, she used to raise some fireworks from that workbench of hers. Remember how we used to spy on her? She knew we were there all along, of course. Oh my God. She had a daughter—what was her name again?"

"Leigh." Jools glanced sideways at me, grinning like an idiot. "You had such a crush on her."

I feigned ignorance. "Did not."

"Oh, horseshit. What were we, thirteen? I had to listen to you every night, waxing on about how good Leigh was at everything from riding a horse to spitting in the dirt."

"Were you jealous?"

Jools smirked. "No."

"Okay, so maybe I had a little crush on her. You know, you really have a talent for making people confess stuff. You should have joined the CIA."

She smiled secretively. "How do you know I haven't?"

There were *oohs* and *aahs* and let's not forget *Oh Katie look how big you've grown!* from Jools's parents. Bless their hearts, but they could go on sometimes. Her father gave us expensive whisky the moment our suitcases were on the floor, then asked whether we'd picked up any hitchhikers along the way. Jools said no, we hadn't because the ghost of Uniondale wasn't a lesbian. Four whiskies and some eggnog later, Jools's mom showed us to the bedroom we'd be sharing. I was the drunkest I'd been on Christmas Eve for a while.

Once we were alone, I opened the big windows that looked out over a vast lawn with stables at the far end. I needed a cigarette to balance out the continuous spinning of my head. The match sparked in the gloomily lit room. A lamp threw a dim glow from a low table in a far corner. Jools handed me an ashtray she found in the drawer of one of the double bed's side tables. She was giggling about something. She too, had had too much to drink.

"What are you on about?" I asked, blowing smoke out the window.

Jools looked at the bed, then at me. Back at the bed again.

"Do you think my parents are trying to give us a subtle hint?"

"What?"

"I think secretly they've always wanted us to get together. It's sort of sweet."

"It's sort of twisted, if you ask me."

"Jools's giggling progressed to an outright drunken laugh, and then she promptly collapsed on the bed.

"Pssst," I heard from her a moment later. "Give me a drag."

"You don't smoke."

"Don't tell me what I do and don't do. Gimme a drag."

I passed her the half-smoked cigarette, and as our fingers briefly touched I felt a surprising current of lust dash through my body. It shocked the hell out of me, and I fumbled in my jacket for another cigarette. Thank God the room was dark.

Jools and I had been friends since primary school, drawn together by our mutual aspiration to not be cool kids. We've seen one another through breakups, breakouts, and break-throughs. Laughed together and cried together; through the thickest of thicks and the thin parts in between. For the better part of eighteen years we have both been too busy finding ourselves to even contemplate the possibility of being *together*. Yet lo and behold—here it was now, cropping up on an unplanned trip, on a farm in the middle of nowhere.

Or was it just me?

"Jools?" I walked from the window over to where she was lying on the bed. Jools was snoring softly. The last bit of the cigarette I had given her smoldered in the ashtray on the edge of the bed. I crunched it out along with mine. Then I carefully rolled Jools to one side of the bed and turned her the right way up. I decided against undressing her. I even decided against undressing myself. I threw the duvet over her, and was thankful that December was one of the hottest months of the year on the African continent. I lay down above the duvet, stiff as a rake, too scared to move, my whole body in a state of flux: excited, scared, confused.

"Ho ho ho!"

I thought I heard the far-off sound of a rather feminine sounding Kris Kringle. Since I was still half asleep though, I thought it might have been the leftover threads of some fantastic Christmas nightmare.

Then: "Ho, ho, *ho*, young lady!"

The shrieks of small children beneath the bedroom window made me sit upright in a hurry, desperate to find out which was the real world.

Oh.

This *was* the real world.

As my eyes adjusted to the sharp morning light, I saw Santa Claus in the doorway, his huge fake gut straining to squeeze through.

"Jools?" I muttered, not sure whether my eyes were playing tricks on me. My mouth felt like a pack of hamsters had taken up residence inside it.

Santa made it through the doorway at last, tripped on a nearby coat hanger, and stumbled right onto me, pressing me back down into the sinking mattress. The shock of the previous night's revelation came right back to me. There was a moment during which I contemplated pulling down Jools's fake beard and kissing her right there. But I resisted. Who wants to be the Grinch who ruined Christmas? I had no idea how she felt. Where the fuck was this coming from, anyway?

"Your gut is suffocating me," I muttered, hoping she would get off me.

"Impressive, isn't it?" Jools smiled in my face. Her beard bobbed up and down as she talked. And she was lying right on top of me as if it didn't matter. I laughed and stuffed my face into the nearest pillow.

"What the hell are you doing?" Jools asked.

"I haven't brushed my teeth."

"Oh my God. You filthy pig." She pulled the pillow out from underneath my face. I seemed to notice for the first time how blue her eyes were. They looked different from so close up. I felt her hips against mine through the heavy material of the Santa suit, and we both stopped laughing. Sun from the window had crept onto the bed.

"Juliet!"

Somewhere down the corridor her mother was calling for her. That, and more shrieks from below the bedroom window brought us to our senses. Jools got up and off me just before her mother appeared in the doorway.

"The children are waiting for Santa to deliver the gifts. Juliet, dear, your beard has gone all askew."

Jools tugged at the suit and adjusted its accessories, not looking at me. "I'll be right there. Why don't you round them all up and park them under the tree?"

"Okeydokey."

I managed to wait until Jools's mother had left the room before a hysterical grunt escaped my throat. "Okeydokey?"

Jools gave me an apologetic look. And then the look turned into something else, but we were both too chicken-shit to say anything.

So it wasn't just me.

I panicked. The first thing I could think to do was to pull the duvet cover over my head. So I did exactly that. And pretended that nothing had happened, while my body wished that Jools was out of that Goddamned suit and underneath the blankets with me.

Of course, I had seen her naked before on plenty of occasions. I couldn't get those glimpses out of my mind now, my memory especially fixated on the white cotton underwear she always favored.

"Fuck. Oh... *fuck*."

I sat on one of the chairs at the back of the expensively furnished yet homely family room.

Watching Santa.

It was exciting and confusingly frightening to see Jools in this new light. I kept wondering what had prevented this from happening before—and then I remembered something. An incident that now flashed in my head liked a fluorescent bulb that needed a good tightening.

It was two years ago, at a farewell party for one of our mutual friends. Granted, we had both been pretty drunk, but we were still lucid enough to know what we were doing. The influence of intoxication was probably how we'd gotten stuck in the bathroom in the first place. One of those difficult door latches. We were locked in for no more than ten minutes, a short time span in which we almost kissed—twice. The second time might well have led to something more, had it not been for that silly bitch Sue Friedman, who managed to open the door right on cue. Jools had been the instigator of both kisses.

Why had we ignored the whole thing? Because we could

lose a friendship? Yet, what had we possibly stood to gain?

Jools ho-ho-hoed her way from one wide-eyed kid to another. A smile crossed my lips when I thought about teasing Jools later that her first appearance in drag had been at her parents'. At Christmas. She looked sexily butch.

The kids would give her a curious glance every so often once they were parked on her knee, but only until she pulled a smartly wrapped gift from beneath the sparkling tree.

"Who else wants to sit on Santa's knee?" Jools boomed theatrically. The floor in front of her was suddenly empty. I looked up to see Mr. and Mrs. Cayce toddling off behind the last of a bunch of very happy kids, shooing the lot outside for lunch on the patio. Jools turned her attention to me.

"How about you, little girl? You've been sitting back there in the corner this whole time."

It was now undeniable. Although we were sitting on opposite sides of the room, there was an unspoken current of electricity between us. A big, fat obvious exclamation point had hit both of us square between the eyes.

"I need a cigarette," I finally said. All the way out the room I could feel Jools's eyes on me. The rush of blood crashed loudly in my ears as I hurried down the long stretch of corridor. That must have been why I didn't hear Jools come down the hallway behind me. When I rushed into the bedroom and turned to close the door, she was there. She'd undone the jacket of the Santa suit, and must have gotten rid of the sponge gut somewhere along the way. All I could think was how hot she looked in a tight little vest and her out-of-place red, rough pants.

"You're not running away from me again, are you?" she asked.

"I need a cigarette," I repeated.

"You need to kiss me," she corrected me, our lips close. And then she did, not waiting any longer for me to respond.

It was slow but certain. How obvious it was then, more than ever—this was something both of us had been contemplating. So much suppressed yearning and lust expressed itself in that kiss that I thought my senses would leave me in a blast of ecstatic overkill.

"Lock the door," I breathed into Jools's mouth. The lock clicked and she was back in my arms before my skin had the chance to miss her warmth. She stealthily backed me up against the wall and our kiss this time was deeper, needier, altogether greedier. My hands were in her strawberry-blonde hair, pulling her closer—so close I thought she'd stepped into me. We certainly weren't behaving like friends anymore. I forgot that we had been.

"The bed…" I wasn't sure which of us had said it, but it sounded like a good idea. I could hardly stand any longer. I gave Jools the chance to slip out of her confining red pants. She wore nothing underneath except for a hot little seventies-inspired bit of lingerie. I pushed her onto the bed and climbed on top of her gorgeous body. She had a washboard stomach, the muscles of which jumped as I traced my hand down her flank. I felt her hands along my back, the tips of her fingers reaching down into the back of my jeans.

We were kissing again. I couldn't seem to stop. Every look she had ever given me replayed itself in my mind with newfound meaning. Every misplaced touch, every nuance of every veiled word. Every urge I'd ever had concerning Jools was flowing through our kisses. Her head was lifting up from the pillow to meet me, her hands traveling down to hold on to my thighs, the tips of her thumbs kneading at the soft, sensitive skin just below my hip bones.

Jools pulled me more tightly to her, our bodies melding into one solid configuration of pleasure. My thigh felt the hot current building up in her—between us. With a rough shove I edged up her hugger of a vest, exposing her breasts. She sat up against the headboard and exhaled loudly, oh so expressively, as I took one of her erect nipples between my lips and sucked.

"This isn't fair," I heard her say. "Kat...take off *your* shirt."

My mouth let go of her reluctantly, only because I was intent on doing anything to please her. My T-shirt landed on the floor and seconds later her hands were on me. Tracing my ribs, cupping my breasts, kneading them softly. Then her legs were clamped round my back, and I could feel her thigh riding up my leg and we were trying to reach each other for another kiss and then the bedpost creaked loudly as Jools said, "In me...."

My hand between her legs seemed to work of its own volition, but it most assuredly registered to my brain how hard she was behind the flexible, slight confines of her sexy underwear.

The air became thick and heavy with our collectively generated heat. We seemed to be moving in slow motion; me looking down at Jools's eyes fluttering every so often behind closed lids, her hips rocking up to meet my hand.

"You're too far away," she said then, and with both hands grabbed handfuls of my jeans and pulled my hips to hers, pushing my fingers skillfully into her to the hilt.

"Fuck...oh, *fuck*—"

And I did; tightly, because she wouldn't let go of me, wouldn't let me remove myself from her so much as an inch, not a stitch. Sweat bound us together; sweat and mutual refusal to risk anything that could disrupt our bliss. She was saying things to me—I forget what. I was only aware of how she began to tighten around my fingers, trying to be quiet in front of the open window, and the way we were looking into one another's eyes, her blue, blue fucking eyes....

And then we were lying in one another's arms, spent, drained—too weak to move. I felt Jools's hand on my naked back, mingling with the touch of the sun. I wondered if her parents had noticed we were missing. I wondered what all our friends would say back home.

But none of that really mattered, because I'd gotten exactly what I wanted for Christmas.

You Better Not Pout
Dante Davidson

"Better not." I glared at her.

She got that worried look in her deep blue eyes, and then she swallowed hard, but her full ruby-slicked bottom lip was stuck firmly in place. Pouting is one of Clarissa's favorite activities. It falls somewhere before shopping for lingerie and after sucking my cock.

"That's not going to win you the necklace," I assured her, gripping her wrist with one hand and dragging her back toward the packed parking structure.

"You're hurting me, Declan," she hissed. "Let go."

"No way, baby. Not after what you just put me through."

I had my hand on my belt before we were even at the car, and I saw Clarissa meekly notice my fingers strumming the pounded silver buckle. Suddenly, there was a true change in her attitude, a complete transformation from the little brat she'd played in the jewelry store—I want *this*. I want *that*—to someone who might realize she had another thing coming. What she *wanted* was a spanking. Maybe she didn't realize that's what she wanted, but I knew the truth.

"Get in," I told her when we finally reached the car at the far end of the lot.

"What are you going to do?" Everything about her demeanor had changed. She seemed shy where before she'd been bold and brassy. Of course, I knew this was simply another one of her many sides. Clarissa has a full range of characters that she can step inside without a problem. But she had a problem now. Me.

"Get in, bend over the seat, and pull up your dress."

"People might see." Her dark eyes were blazing now, a perfect blue. They matched the color in the necklace she had so admired.

"You should have thought about that before you pulled your spoiled brat routine," I told my gorgeous, leggy girlfriend. "You shouldn't have pushed me like that, Clara."

"I—" she stuttered, apparently realizing that I wasn't kidding. "I didn't mean to—"

That was a lie, and we both knew it. She meant everything, every fucking thing. "Quiet," I demanded. "Bend over the backseat. Lift your dress. If you make me wait even one more second, I'll do it for you. And if I have to do it for you, those panties are coming down, too."

"*What* panties?"

The way she said the words made my throat tighten. Oh, Christ, the bad girl. She'd gone out into the mass of holiday shoppers without her knickers on. For the past several hours, as we'd made our way from crowded store to crowded store, she'd had a sexy secret. All those little smiles she'd shot me,

the lustful looks that I'd taken for granted, had all been because of this sexy secret. When she'd reached her limits, she'd
orchestrated the whole thing in the jewelry store to get a rise
out of me. Well, her plan had worked. She'd gotten a rise, all
right. Both out of my temper, and out of my cock.

And now she was going to pay.

I didn't have to tell her again to assume the position. She
bent over and slowly raised the hem of her red velvet dress.
It was a short dress, one of my favorites. Very festive, very
tiny. As she pulled the hem higher and higher, I saw that
she'd been telling the truth: there were no panties waiting
underneath that hem. Nothing but pure, seemingly endless
skin. I pulled my belt free while I watched her, knowing that
I'd better put the play into motion before I came right there,
next to the car, where some bundled-up matron with her
arms loaded with overpriced crap might see me.

When Clara had her dress bunched up to her waist, I
doubled the belt and let it smack against her naked skin. She
let out a little yelp, but then wriggled her curvy hips at me,
clearly urging me to hit her again and to do so harder. I didn't
hesitate to fulfill her needs. I slapped the black leather against
her skin a second time, watching the pale raspberry mark
bloom there, and my cock gave another dangerous throb in
my jeans. I'd been picturing this very scenario since she'd
first told me we were going Christmas shopping this morning. Because for Clara, shopping for gifts always includes gifts
for herself. And when I'm around, she loves to employ her
bratty little girl routine. She knows it will get her something
she wants—whether it's the gift in question, or a scene like
this, she'll take what she can get.

I slapped her ass several more times with the hide of my
belt, realizing as I did so that I would be happy to keep this

up all afternoon. The sound was thrilling to me, as always, and the way Clara kept shimmying her ass in between blows made me light-headed with desire. But we were in public now, and I couldn't afford much more time. At any moment, we might be caught, and I was fairly sure that our antics would not be approved by any mall-sanctioned security guard. Sure, this was helping *my* holiday mood, but others might not share my belief in what the holidays are truly all about.

Done spanking her, at least for the moment, I pushed her roughly forward even further into the car and tore open my jeans. My cock was as ready as it's ever been. I'd known from the moment she first pulled her act as Miss Brat that this would be the end result, but I hadn't known exactly how excited the whole spectacle would make me. As I gripped her hips and thrust my cock inside of her, she made the sweetest whimpering noise ever. I looked at her face, turned sideways against the leather seat, and I saw that her pretty pout had been replaced by a look of pure pleasure.

Quickly, I slid one hand under her body and began to strum my fingers against her clit, all the while pounding into her with my cock. She moaned softly, and I kept up my fingering games, thrusting into her while teasing her clit in the sweetest way imaginable. The heat from her ass radiated outward, and I knew that each forward push of my body against hers reminded her of her most recent spanking.

When she came, she let me know by the contractions of her pussy around my cock, and by the soft purring sounds her breath made. I came a second after her, and then pulled out and changed my position so I could cradle her on my lap in the backseat, our clothes in disarray, but our bodies aligned. Gazing down at her, I saw that longing in her blue eyes yet again. She wanted more. Just as she always does, hungry little thing. She tilted her head to look at me, bee-stung lips already pursed.

"Better not," I whispered to her before she could say a word. "Better not even think about it." But both of us knew better. I can never deny Clara what she really and truly wants. And by the time we got home, I knew that her pretty pout was going to get her exactly what she wanted all over again.

Santa's Favorite Elf
Molly Laster

The Private Panty in West Hollywood caters mostly to women, drag queens, and transvestites. We sell lingerie in an extraordinary range of sizes and fabrics: rubber, vinyl, plastic wrap—you name it, we've carried it. Holidays are our biggest time, sales-wise. On Valentine's Day, we sell out of everything red. Around Halloween, we can't keep black on the racks. For Christmas, we do a fair business, too. I should know. I play Santa.

If you drive by Santa Monica and Palm anytime after Thanksgiving, you can see me in the window, clad in red vinyl with a big black belt around my slim waist and a pair of the meanest boots in existence. While shoppers browse the racks, I take customers on my knee and ask them what they want for Christmas.

Of course, bad little shoppers go over my knee, instead of

on it, for a quick demonstration of our various punishment implements. If you're a bad little girl, these are the things you hope to find under your tree on Christmas morning: leather-covered paddles, English-made riding crops, bone-crafted canes.

This year, the lines to meet with Santa grew so long that our manager hired a new employee, Sara, to play Santa's Elf. She was set up in a chair in our opposite window, and when I took my breaks, I'd watch her in action.

You've probably guessed that we don't get many nice shoppers: the people who visit with Santa are *all* naughty. Sara, clad in black vinyl with a red belt, her long, black hair pulled back, her dark eyes flashing, paddled many a shopper to tears while I watched…and felt something stir inside me.

I've read that many doms need an occasional taste of punishment themselves. After an eleven P.M. closing on Christmas Eve, I decided it was my turn. While Sara was still seated in the window, I asked if she'd do me a favor. When she nodded, waiting to hear me spill it, I climbed over her lap and confessed my sins.

She didn't need any more encouragement than that. In a flash, I felt the sting of a paddle against my vinyl-clad ass. I have a high pain tolerance, but she had me squirming and whimpering in no time. Then, without a word, she shoved me off her lap and into the fake snow, unzipping the fly on her vinyl pants and yanking them down.

"Service me," she said, softly tugging on my hair to pull me forward. "Get me off."

I needed no more instruction. I moved forward on my hands and knees and pressed my lips to her shaved cunt. She was warm from being encased in vinyl all day, and her job had apparently turned her on. There was a pool of glossy cum trapped between her thighs. I was quick to lap it up, quicker still to probe her deeply with my tongue, to get my hands into the action and work her.

"We have an audience…," she murmured, and I turned my head slightly to see a late-evening crowd of partiers watching the show. It didn't stop me. I continued until she was moaning, until she had pressed her body against the window—mooning the crowd—and was gripping me to her with fingers like death.

Her cunt tasted like sugarplums, like peppermint candy, like something I've dreamed of but never experienced. Her juices flowed from her sopping pussy into my mouth, drenching my lips, my chin, and my cheeks. I was in ecstasy.

But when she creamed, rocking against me with the rhythmic beating of her orgasm, I pulled back, startled.

"Did you hear that?" I asked.

She shook her head, her dark hair falling free of its band and cascading forward over her flushed cheeks.

"That sound…like bells?"

"I heard bells all right," she said, laughing, pulling up her suit.

For a moment, I'd thought that I'd heard the *real* Santa, the hooves of the reindeer, the deep jolly laugh. For a moment, I found that I actually still believed. But then I shook my head to clear the crazy thought and gave Sara a quick Christmas kiss. She flushed and handed me a present that had been hidden under her chair. I took it home to place beneath my tree. Or, rather, *we* took it home together, because she came right along with me.

I guess that sometimes it pays to be naughty.

Bound for Bodie
Simon Sheppard

Winter in the mountains is always brutal, brutal as Hell. You never do get used to it, you never do forget it. I left godless Bodie many years back, but those whiteout Decembers still whistle through my bones, bitter and barren. There was only one reason to be in that Helldorado, and that was the Standard Mine and the gold it brought up from the cold, hard ground. The gold that we long-suffering miners brought up, day after backbreaking, perilous day.

My last Christmas Eve there was clear and windy, so cold you couldn't stay outside for more than a few minutes, lest the wind off the mountains freeze your flesh and steal your life. So we wrapped ourselves up as best we could and hurried on over to the Royal Flush Saloon, our boots crunching through the crusty snow.

At the best of times, even Easter Sunday morning, the

Royal Flush was a rough and rowdy place, but on the eve of Our Savior's nativity—the next day being a respite from work—every man was raising Perdition itself. By the time me and my buddies get there, all and sundry are roaring drunk and the whores are doing turn-away business.

Comes to that, Madame Mustache, one of the gurdy girls, is leaning right up against the bar with her hand down the front of Cal Callahan's pants. And Cal, who's slugging down the panther piss, doesn't seem to mind at all when Madame Mustache, in front of everyone and God, unbuttons his fly and just pulls out the thing itself and works it hard. As the piano rolls and the whiskey flows, me and my three best comrades get hot, hotter, and horny as God and the angels.

"Let's get us some cunt," says Lefty.

"Looks like all the cunt is busy," Hiram tells him.

"Well then, fuck 'em, let's dance," Lefty roars, downing another shot.

So we choose for who's going to be girls and Hiram and me tie kerchiefs 'round our arms since we're to be the ladies this time, and off we go, Hiram in Lefty's arms and Texas Joe leading me. The dance floor was crowded, almost all men, excepting for two or three crib girls taking a break from their duties upstairs.

Texas Joe's a nice enough fellow, although always horny and he never takes a bath. And tonight Texas Joe's getting real drunk, indeed. While we're whirling around the jam-packed salon, he grabs my ass and holds me close and then closer, and tarnation if he doesn't have a big stiff one that he keeps jamming up against me, rubbing that thing on my leg like he's some mangy dog, which in a manner of speaking he is.

"Holy Hell," Texas Joe says, "I'm so fucking horny I

could fuck a handful of mud. If it wasn't all frozen fucking solid." He laughs. He's got me held tight against him now, and there might be some folks who would mind, prudes and good Christians and such, but late Christmas Eve at the Royal Flush, there's no one around who could give a fuck. And the truth of it is that I stumbled onto Texas Joe jacking off one summer's night behind the tailings, and he's got a nice big rod that I figure would be mighty fine to fool around with.

So I say, "Hey, Texas Joe, all the whores are busy and I bet nobody's back at the lodging house. So why don't you and me head on back and I'll give you what you need."

"For real?"

"For real."

"Well, MERRY FUCKING CHRISTMAS!"

"Merry Fucking Christmas!" some of the other miners yell back as Texas Joe drags me out the door.

By the time we get to in front of the church, Texas Joe's staggering badly, but nonetheless, he's got a hot hand down the front of my trousers, working my balls into a lather. For someone who's always loudly proclaiming his love of snatch, Texas Joe sure knows how to give a hand job, but then I reckon he should know how, since he's always practicing on himself. Shit, I'd like to get down on my knees and blow him right there, but his big, frozen thing would probably snap off in my mouth like an icicle.

So I'm thinking not-unpleasant thoughts about big Texas Joe getting me under his hairy, smelly body, when all of a sudden he grunts and falls facedown in the snow, sprawled out unconscious in the doorway of the church.

"C'mon, Texas Joe," I say, "we got to get you inside where it's warm." I struggle to get him to his feet, but my boots keep sliding in the snow, and my poor hands are like to freeze.

"Can I help?" asks a voice, and I look up to see a finely-dressed young gentleman with hair the color of summer wheat. His eyes meet mine, and when they do he gives a little shiver.

So then he takes one arm and I take the other and we push and drag Texas Joe till we get him back to the miners' lodging house, which is plumb empty on account of all the boys being out raising Hell. When we get him dumped into his filthy bed, my newfound helper smiles and says, "My name is Lars."

"Well, Lars," I say, after offering my name, "thank you most kindly for helping me get Texas Joe back here." At which moment, as though he heard himself mentioned, Joe belches loudly and commences to drool on the mattress. Lars, still smiling, says to me, "Surely you won't want to spend the night here." Sniffing the scent of reeking Texas Joe, I can only agree. "Why not come back to my room at the Grand Central Hotel?" The Grand Central being the most high-class lodging that Bodie has to offer.

"Thank you kindly, Mr. Lars, but I was figuring I'd go back and carouse at the Royal Flush awhile."

"I'm not much of a drinking man myself," says he, "but perhaps you could walk me back to my hotel and then be on your way."

So we set off from the reeking lodging house, and as we hurry over the board sidewalks, my companion tells me how he came to be in Bodie. He was born in Norway, son of an already-wealthy father whose investments in the Standard Mining Company had lately repaid him manyfold. Whilst his father counted his money in his fine new San Francisco mansion, Lars was sent out to oversee the vicissitudes of the family's business. He'd lately spent time in Leadville, and then the Comstock, before making his way to Bodie, which he reached in December, right before the Great Storm crashed down upon us, stranding all of us and killing a few.

As we near the Grand Central Hotel, whoops and hollers from the nearby saloons rend the freezing air. In the near distance, in front of the Bella Union Gambling House, where us miners play faro and Spanish monte until dawn, two men are having a fight; it was only the next day that I learned that Tom Dillon had stabbed Thomas Travis to death, and that the dying Travis, for his part, raised his pistol and shot his assailant clean through the heart.

The Grand Central Hotel is as fine a place as I've ever been in. The lobby's ablaze with lights, a well-decorated pine tree in every corner, and the splendid dining hall is filled with well-dressed celebrants. One angelic little girl, no older than ten, is standing upon a table, leading the multitude in a chorus of "Oh, Holy Night." It is certainly not in no wise the Royal Flush.

The desk clerk, nose in the air, looks at me like he knows I don't belong, but changes his tune when Lars says, "He's with me," and slips him a shiny silver dollar.

"So, my friend, can I not invite you up to my rooms to drink a holiday toast?" And indeed, when he looks at me with his piercing blue eyes, it seems a fair enough prospect.

Reappearing moments later, a glass of champagne in each hand, he leads me up the sweeping staircase and shows me into his lodgings.

His room is cold, so he feeds the stove before we raise our glasses and toast the birthday of Our Lord. When we've drained our glasses dry, he says, "It still is mighty cold in here.

Perhaps we can share the bed until the room is warmer."

Without another word he removes his expensive calfskin boots and I follow suit and soon we're lying face-to-face on the starched white sheets of the feather bed, beneath the heaped-up blankets. I can feel his breath upon me as he reaches up to stroke my face. Oh how my heart does beat!

"There is something I have not yet told you," he says softly to me. "When I was in Leadville, some bandits robbed the mining office whilst I worked there. As they went about their dirty business, they took lengths of rope and tied me firmly to a chair so that I could not interfere. I was frightened, of course, but also strangely excited by the experience."

I did not yet see why he chose this time to tell me this tale.

"And since then…" He hesitates. "Since then I have been wanting to relive that day, to be tied up again by a strong, rough man…a man like you."

As he speaks these words, my loins stir to their fullest extent.

"But we haven't the ropes and gear," I say.

"Oh, but we do, in that traveling bag over there. I've tried using them upon myself, but it hasn't been near the same."

Well sir, as you can imagine, I get up and open the luggage, which contains a large quantity of rope, as well as some leather straps and thongs. I had never heard an odder request in all my days, but I was surely game to give it a go.

"Sit in that chair over there." Which he does with alacrity. He closes his eyes and is unmoving, breathing nervously. Standing behind the chair, I roughly pull his hands behind the chair's back, wrapping a rope several times around his trembling wrists, securing it with a square knot. As he makes no complaint, I take one of the straps and draw it around his upper arms, pulling it tight and buckling it, so's his chest is thrust forward. At this he begins to moan softly.

"Did I hurt you?" I ask.

"Not at all. Not at all," says he. "I beg you continue."

So I kneel to remove his stockings, rolling up his trouser legs to expose his pale ankles. I grab one naked foot and lift it off the ground, using a rope to secure it to a rung of the chair. I tie the other smooth, bare foot to the chair, leaving his knees spread wide. Already, he's pretty damn helpless, but I take another rope and wind it around his thighs. I can't help but notice the stiff bulk of his John Thomas pressing up against the fabric of his trousers.

When I've made sure that the rope securing his thighs to the chair is good and tight, I stand back to admire my handiwork. He's trussed up pretty good, straining against the ropes and groaning. You can see just by looking in his eyes that he's plumb hungry for it.

"I could do just about anything to you that I wanted, couldn't I?" I say with a growl. "Anything I wanted." And this, rather than frightening him, only seems to excite him all the more. I rip open the buttons of his shirt. His pale white chest exposed to me, I run my hands over the golden hairs till I feel his nipples, and I give them a fearsome tweaking. He jumps at first, but as I squeeze harder yet, he whispers fervently, "Oh, yes!"

Reaching down, I unbuckle his belt and pull open his trousers. The shape of his stiff rod is shown plainly through the flannel of his underwear, and when I free it from its constraints, it leaps up quite boldly, a pearl of moisture at its pointy tip.

"Time to truss you up real good, I reckon," I say, which brings a smile to his pretty lips. I use a long piece of rope to fasten his torso to the chair, wrapping it around and around, tightening it so that the rope presses firmly against the bare flesh of his chest.

Then I get a leather thong out of the bag and slowly wind it around the base of his hard rod, going around the base of his balls till the sack is stretched out pretty good, then wrapping it around the shaft till it's all nicely tied up. I then take the end of that long thong and secure it to a coat hook on the wall opposite, so his privates are cruelly stretched out and under constant tension.

"That should hold you," says I, walking out the door.

I go downstairs, past the sniffy clerk, and out into the frozen, moonlit night. Within several minutes I'm back at the Royal Flush, where the party has gotten even wilder. Lefty's sprawled in a corner, a drunken whore on his lap, him working his hand up under her skirts, while Hiram is being whirled 'round the floor by big Owen, the blacksmith. I go over to Hiram and speak loudly, so as to be heard above the tumult.

"So you haven't had a turn with one of the girls yet, Hiram?"

"No, I ain't," says Hiram, voice slurred with whiskey, "and I'm Goddamn horny as all Hell." He reaches down and gives his substantial crotch a squeeze.

"Well, come with me then, for I've got a pleasant surprise for you, a Christmas gift, as t'were."

We're back at the Grand Central Hotel several minutes later, and this time the desk clerk doesn't even look our way. When I fling open the door to Lars's room, Hiram is surely surprised. "Well, I'll be damned! What the Hell?"

"I've roped this critter and now I mean to ride him. Care to join me?"

Well, sir, Lars was sitting there with a real dreamy look

on his face, softly straining against the ropes that held him to the chair, and that long prong of his was still hard as ore-bearing rock.

"Shit, let's get him onto the bed," says Hiram.

So we untie him and, Hiram at his head and me at his feet, carry him over to the four-poster.

"Heads up or facedown?" asks Hiram.

"Heads up. At first."

We get him stretched out on the bed and tie his wrists and ankles to the bedposts, tugging now and then to make sure his naked body is good and taut.

"You ready to be ridden, rich boy?"

"Oh, Jesus, Mary, and Joseph," moans Lars, "I'm more than ready."

So Hiram and I pull down our britches. I guess I shouldn't be surprised that Hiram's big red cock is stiff and ready for action. "You want him first?" he asks. I tell him to go on ahead. With a grunt, he climbs up on the bed, straddles Lars's chest, and slips his big bone into the Norwegian's open mouth, pumping himself into his throat.

Meantime, I spit into my hand and wet down my fingers real good, then reach up between the blond's slender thighs, fingering apart the cheeks of his butt till I feel the heat of his tight hole. He presses down onto my fingers, taking two of them deep inside. As I drive them home, his trussed-up dick jumps and starts oozing juice.

"Tarnation, this feels good," Hiram moans, hairy buttocks pumping as he slides in and out of the boy's mouth. I lick a finger of my free hand, get it good and wet, and slide it down the crack of Hiram's ass. The muscles resist at first, but soon my finger is deep inside, and it just makes Hiram even lustier.

When he looks over his shoulder, Hiram's all red in the face. "I feel like I'm going to spew my jissom any time now. If you want to flip him over, we'd best do it now."

I slide my fingers out of both men's asses and Hiram pulls out of the boy's mouth. We untie Lars from the bedposts and get him onto his belly. Lying facedown in the lantern light, his pale naked body looks like drifts of snow.

"Lift up your fucking head," Hiram says, and he's at the head of the bed, legs spread wide, Lars's head between his big, hairy thighs. "Now suck on me some more." Which the blond man does, without hesitation.

I cinch Lars's wrists and ankles back again to the bedposts, then lower myself down between his spread-eagle legs and ease myself into his butt, the red-hot, wet pleasure of it. I pump away into him, enjoying the sight of the coils of rope that wind 'round his wrists, that press into his smooth, white flesh.

And just then a tremendous ruckus erupts outside, men firing guns into the air and hollering "Merry Christmas!" Hiram grabs Lars's fine blond head in both calloused hands and pushes it hard into his crotch as he shoots off into the rich boy's throat. And I, seeing the look on Hiram's face, can hold back no more, and plow a load deep into that snowy ass.

Well, as you can imagine, it takes a minute for us all to catch our breath, and then Lars looks up, spunk still dripping from the corner of his mouth, and smiles. "Merry Christmas, boys." A big ol' wet grin.

At that I suddenly feel kind of melancholy, remembering the folks I'd left behind when I came to Bodie. Here it is Christmas, and here we all are in a lawless, Godforsaken hole, colder than Hell, far from family and childhood friends. But then I look at Lars and Hiram, and I can't help but grin, too.

I get up and peer through the lace curtains, out at the million stars in the cold winter sky, and think of that one star so long ago. And then Lars, newly untied, comes up behind me and, pressing against me, throws his fair arms about my waist, and my pecker rises again.

And I muse that Easter springtime's not so far off, after all.

'Tis the Season
Eric Williams

'Tis the season, or so the tinned holiday music keeps telling me. 'Tis the season to be jolly. Fa la fucking la, la, la,
la, la. And I don't mean to sound clichéd here, or anything
like Scrooge, but I'm not the slightest bit into the Christmas
spirit. I can't take the music. I can't stand the fruitcake. And
if someone tries to pass me another cup of frigging eggnog,
I'm going to go fucking nuts. Who invented eggnog? What
moron decided that raw egg mixed with rum, cream, and
nutmeg equalled holiday heaven? *Please.* Give me a good old
bottle of Pilsner any day of the week.

I'm sick of women with the tinkling jingle bell ear-
rings—green in one ear, red in the other. I'm sick of mistletoe dangling dangerously from every archway. If I'm going
to kiss someone, I want to do it on my own desire, not because I'm standing under a weed. And I'm supremely sick of

holiday-themed everything: Holiday scented potpourri. Holiday scented soap. Holiday scented shampoo, I swear to fucking God. Some chick at my office—and, yes, I know it was a chick because no guy would ever buy this—actually gave me body wash that smells like gingerbread. I couldn't even force my face into a smile. Yeah, she was my secret Santa. And yeah there was a price limit on the gifts. But I'm a man, for Christ's sake. Why on earth would I want to smell like a cookie?

To be fair, the bottle *was* sort of cool, from some brand called Philosophy, which I'd never heard of. They don't make things like that for men. Or at least not men like me who tend to buy all the toiletries we need at a five-and-dime, not an upscale department store. One of the other ladies in the office made a sort of "ooh" noise when I opened it, and I could tell that she wanted to trade what she'd gotten. Curious, I glanced over to see what that gift might be, and suddenly found myself slightly more open to the spirit of giving. She was holding a pair of leopard-print cuffs, and she was blushing fiercely, as well.

"Some kinky secret Santa you got," I said, almost under my breath. But she heard me and looked up, then took a step closer. I recognized her as a fellow cube-dweller, one who had only been in the office for a few weeks. I didn't even know her name yet, but I had noticed that she was one of the few women in the joint who hadn't sported battery-operated light-up sweaters or glittery "holiday" eye makeup. One of the few who didn't smell like a candy cane or think it fucking adorable to wear stacks of circular peppermint sticks as bracelets and silver tinsel as hair ornaments. To some, the holidays are open season for displaying bad personal taste.

"Yeah," she said softly. "Pretty kinky, I guess."

"Probably from Shayna in the art department. She wears leopard-print outfits every single day."

"You think?" she asked, and she turned her head to look over at Shayna, who was wearing leopard print this evening, as well, although her outfit tonight was red and green leopard print. Extra festive.

"Why?" I asked. "Who was your guess?"

Her blush darkened, a pretty holly-berry color. "Well, you know. Actually, I thought it was from you—"

Now, I took another moment to look her over, and when someone passed an eggnog my way, I didn't push it aside. "Naw," I said, unable to hide my grin. "I wouldn't have thought of something like that."

"So what *did* you put under the tree?"

"You don't want to know."

She glanced at the different gifts clutched in people's hands, looking back at me in between moments of surveillance. I watched her over the rim of my eggnog cup, wondering if she'd guess correctly.

"Not the fuzzy mouse that plays 'Jingle Bell Rock' when you rub his tummy."

I didn't even have to say no.

"Not the light-up Rudolph nose or the furry brown antlers."

"Uh-uh."

Again, she surveyed the gifts that had been opened, and then she suddenly broke into a grin. "The coal?"

I nodded.

"Is it *really* coal?"

"No, it's black licorice. I couldn't resist."

"So what do you have against Christmas?" she asked, moving even closer to me. "You're not one of those people who thinks it's all overcommercialized and we should get back into the *real* spirit, or anything, are you?"

"Do you mean am I religious freak? No, I have no problem with people bowing down to Santa as their Savior. I just don't like anyone telling me that I have to be jolly."

Again, she gazed at me forcefully, and I could feel her eyes on my body: flat stomach, broad chest. "Yeah, you don't really have that jolly look about you."

"I don't like people telling me much of anything," I confessed.

"Really?" her blue eyes seemed to light up. She took another step closer and I realized I could have put my arms around her trim waist and held her tight to me. Nobody would have even noticed. Where was the mistletoe when you needed it? The buzz had grown louder around us now that the silly gift-opening ceremony was over. People were definitely on their way past tantalizingly tipsy to all-out drunk. "What if someone told you to meet her in the back supply room?"

"Oh," I said, suddenly feeling a bit more jolly than I had before the party started. "Oh, well that would be different. Because that's more of a suggestion, not a command."

"Really?" she asked again. "I'd consider it a command if I were you."

You know, jolliness was now pretty much spreading throughout my body.

"Now?" I asked.

"You don't have a problem being told?" she teased.

I shook my head.

"Now," she agreed, and I set my eggnog down on the nearest desk and followed her around the corner and down the hall. There was some moron from accounting making photocopies of his ass in the copy room, but the supply room at the far end of the hall was empty and dark, except for a strand of tiny twinkling white Christmas lights.

"What if someone told you to put your wrists behind your back," she said now, closing the door behind us.

I did it without a word of protest.

"And get down on your knees."

Did that, too.

"And open your mouth."

I was on my knees, with my hands behind my back and my mouth open, before I could even figure out how I'd gotten there. The pretty blonde quickly used the cuffs on me, and then she stood in front of me and slowly raised her short, dark velvety skirt.

"What about you?" I somehow managed to say. "Why are you wearing black to a holiday party? What do *you* have against Christmas?"

"Nothing," she assured me. "I just happen to agree with you. Forced glee has a way of making me slightly nauseous. That and fruitcake. I like to create my own moods."

"And what sort of mood is this one?"

She pressed the back of my head, forcing my face against her panties and I breathed in deeply, inhaling a scent that I found much more arousing than gingerbread.

"An X-rated Xmas mood," she said, and even in the dimly lit room, when I looked up, I could see the grin on her face. But I didn't have the chance to look up for long. Her fingers twined in my hair, and she pressed me once again into her panties. I kissed her through the shiny fabric, and then started to lick in slow, sexy circles.

She sighed as I worked her, and then swiftly slipped her panties to the left, exposing her smoothly shaved pussy.

I licked harder now, barely keeping my balance on my knees, wanting to lean into her, to fuck her forcefully with my tongue. She held me steady, hands still in my hair, and ground herself against my face as I licked and sucked and nibbled. This was my idea of a Christmas dinner. The perfect way to end a holiday fiesta. I wanted to make her come, and I did my best, off balance, but ever ready to please. Until suddenly, she pulled me back off her and whipped out the key to the cuffs.

"You're releasing me?" I didn't like the thought of it.

"No way," she said. "I'm *repositioning* you." And she quickly captured my hands once again, this time in front of my body. While I watched, she slid her skirt and panties all the way off, then bent over the corner table. I scrambled to undo my slacks with my hands cuffed together, but I somehow managed, freeing my cock and plunging into her. She lifted her hips to help me and I drove inside, actually fucking her to the tune of "Here Comes Santa Claus" playing mercilessly in the other room.

In that twinkling light, everything seemed magical. The way she moved beneath me. The way her hair took on a glistening sheen. And for the first time since the holidays had come upon us—way back sometime in August, I think—I found myself at peace. This was what the holidays were truly about. Connecting. Rejoicing. Finding total pleasure with your fellow man—or, in this case, woman.

She came first, groaning beneath me, and I followed a beat later, biting into her shoulder as I climaxed, sure that I had torn the thin fabric of her slippery black silk top, but not caring at all. I pressed her against the table for a final moment, breathing hard, and then rolled off her and awkwardly tried to pull up my slacks. When she undid my wrists a second time and started playing with the cuffs, herself, I had a fresh image of Christmas joy instantly in my mind: this pretty vixen cuffed to my desk chair while I fucked her. Or bent over the photocopy machine, if the nimrod from accounting was finished with it.

"So you really think these were from Shayna?" she asked.

"I don't know. That was just my first thought." I hesitated, looking at her and at the dangerous gleam in her clear blue eyes. "Why?"

"Cause we could go snag her and invite her to join us. I mean, if you'd like—"

All of a sudden I realized that my pitiful thoughts about the misery of the holidays had all but disappeared. And as I opened the door and peered down the hall at the partying staff in the main room, I couldn't help but think: 'Tis the fucking season. That's for sure.

Holly
JT Langdon

It was a slow night. Most girls wouldn't even bother working on Christmas Eve. But I had nothing else to do. Might
as well turn a couple of tricks, right? I stood on the corner
of Cermak and Wentworth just across from the entrance to
Chinatown freezing my butt off. What choice did I have?
Potential customers wouldn't see the merchandise if I was
wrapped in a parka. It wasn't that bad. I had on a faux-mink
coat over my halter top and leather miniskirt. Sheer black
hose tucked into knee-high leather boots kept my legs warm.
At least it wasn't snowing.

   I liked working Chinatown. On regular nights the air
was sweet from the Chinese restaurants that lined either side
of Wentworth, and when things got slow or the cops were
out in numbers I could walk down the street and look in the
windows of all the little shops. Not tonight, though. The

streets were eerily silent. Chinatown was a long strip of darkness framed with carved wooden dragons and a pagoda. The air was so cold I could smell it.

Headlights splashed over me as a car rounded the corner. I felt the usual moment of uneasiness all the girls feel at first. Would it be a cop there to roust me? It's part of the trade. Sometimes the cops are just looking for a little quick action. I've given more than a few blowjobs to keep my ass out of jail. When I saw that it wasn't a squad car at the corner I breathed a little easier. Unless the Chicago cops were driving silver BMWs I was okay for now. The car slowed down and for a moment I was hopeful. I had visions of being able to go out to dinner on Christmas Day, or maybe buying myself a new outfit as a gift.

But then the BMW sped off down Cermak. Damn.

I huddled in the doorway of the closed Chinese place behind me to escape a gust of arctic wind. If a john didn't come around soon I would probably give up and go home. Home. For some reason I thought that should have been something nicer on Christmas Eve than the shit hole I lived in. Maybe it was better than nothing. Maybe not. But it was mine. Some girls didn't even have that much. But if that made me lucky, life was pretty sad.

The BMW came around the corner again. It might have been a different one, but how many silver BMWs were driving around Chinatown on Christmas Eve? Maybe someone was having second thoughts. The BMW rolled to a stop at the curb. It sat there for a moment with the motor purring, then the passenger-side door opened a crack. I put on my best smile and walked over to the car, pushing the door open and ducking my head so I could peer inside.

I didn't get a lot of janes, and never ones this attractive.

The woman in the BMW could have been on either side of forty. Though not much, either way. Under her leather duster she wore a red turtleneck sweater and black pants. Her long, dark hair was pinned up and managed to look simple and stylish. No makeup. But then she didn't really need it. The woman smiled at me.

"You look cold standing out there," she said.

I smiled. "Bet you could think of ways to warm me up."

"Yes."

"I charge more to do women."

The woman in the BMW gave a slight nod. "Will five hundred be enough?"

I tried to keep the surprise from my face. She didn't need to know that was twice what I would have asked. It was Christmas. And she offered, right? Besides, she looked like she could afford it. I answered her by getting in the car.

The woman smiled at me then drove off down Cermak. I looked around the interior of the BMW. It was nice just like it was supposed to be. Genuine leather seats. She liked leather. Good. The heat inside the car felt nice to me after being outside all night. She had the radio on but turned down low, Christmas music playing softly. Now that I could see her up close the woman looked more on the other side of forty. But still good. Oh yes. She still looked very, very good.

"I have a place," I said.

"So do I," she said. "Unless you're nervous about going home with me?"

I shook my head. She didn't make me nervous. And for some reason I didn't want her to see the place I usually take tricks. It was too shabby and embarrassed me. What did it matter? She knew what I was. Maybe I thought she deserved better than to fuck a whore in a cheap bed on Christmas Eve.

"You married?" I asked.

She laughed. "Why would you think that?"

"Most of the women I get are married," I said, shrugging. "They want to experiment. You know, satisfy their curiosity."

That made her laugh again. It was a melodic laugh, pretty, filling the car like the scent of perfume lingering in the air. "I've never been able to satisfy that particular curiosity, nor would I ever want to. And no, I am not married."

"So what's your story, then?"

Her gaze never left the road but I could hear the smile in her voice. "You are inquisitive. Does it matter?"

"No. Not really." I could see Lake Michigan up ahead, a giant black pool that made it hard to tell where the water stopped and the sky began. It looked like God had spilled a bottle of ink and never bothered to clean up the mess.

"What's your name?"

"Holly," I said.

"Is that your real name or is it just seasonal?"

"Does it matter?"

She laughed that pretty laugh of hers and I wanted to wrap myself up in it like it was a blanket. "No. Not really."

We drove for a while in near silence except for the Christmas music. The heater whirred softly.

"You're very pretty, Holly." She reached over and slid her hand up my thigh. Did she like the hose? Or would she have preferred bare skin? I would have taken the hose off in the car if she asked me to. For five hundred dollars I would have done just about anything she asked me to. She slid her hand back and forth like she was petting me but never slipped under my skirt.

"What's your name?" I asked.

"Nora."

It fit her like an evening glove. I said, "You're very pretty, too."

It wasn't long before she was unlocking the door and ushering me into her condo on the ninth floor of a high-rise on Lake Shore Drive. The living room was done in shades of brown except for the carpet, which was thick and white. Like snow. Sliding glass doors opened onto a small terrace that must have given Nora a great view of Lake Michigan the rest of the year. Right now, though, she had a Christmas tree set up in front of the doors. Presents were stacked up around the base. Red and green and white lights blinked on and off. The smell of pine was in the air.

"What are you thinking about?"

I turned to her. She had taken off her black leather jacket while I gaped at the posh condo. The red turtleneck really showed off the roundness of her breasts, not too large, but not small, either. Perfect. Would she want me to kiss them, suck on her nipples? I bet she had nice plump nipples. But I wouldn't tell her I was thinking that.

"You," I answered truthfully.

Nora smiled at that. She closed the distance between us in a graceful, sweeping movement, then pulled me into her arms and brushed her lips over mine. It was a soft kiss, much too soft to be wasted on a whore like me. Kisses like that were meant for lovers. I cupped her breast and squeezed it through her thick winter sweater. Nora moaned like she laughed and it had the same affect on me. She pulled back slightly, breathing hard, our lips still very close.

"What do you want me to do?" I asked softly.

"Are you in a hurry?"

I was, actually. But not like she meant it. She thought I

wanted to get it over with and move on to my next john. But really I was in a hurry to see her naked, to get my mouth around her luscious breasts, to fuck her.

"No," I said

Nora smiled against my lips, clearly pleased. "The guest room has its own connecting bath. Why don't you take a nice hot shower?"

"Okay," I said.

The guest room was just down the hall, first door on my right. It was plain compared to the rest of the condo, but it was still nicer than where I lived. The bedcovers were in shades of red. Pink sheets. Maroon comforter. Rose throw pillows. Was that where Nora was going to fuck me, there under the pink sheets instead of in her own bed? It made no difference to me. Did it?

I took off my clothes and piled them on the dresser, then padded naked into the bathroom. It didn't have a bathtub, just a shower stall large enough for two people. There were neatly folded towels, fluffy and white, next to the sink. I ran the hot water. Swirls of steam filled the room like ghosts, floating aimlessly through the air.

The hot water felt wonderful pounding against my naked skin. I soaped up my body, making myself fresh for Nora, and wondered what she was doing while I showered. Did it turn her on to know I was in there? Maybe this was part of the game for her. She could be in the other room getting off while she thought about me in her guest shower, all naked and wet and lathered up.

I got out of the shower, dried myself off with one towel and wrapped another around me, then went back into the guest room. There was a present on the bed, a rectangular gift box wrapped in green paper with a large red bow on it and a card that had FOR HOLLY written on it in sweeping cursive as if done with an old-fashioned quill. I ripped off the wrapping paper like I was a little kid and opened the box. Inside was a red kimono with a narrow black sash. But it wasn't like those cheap ones sold in Chinatown to the tourists. I put it on. The silk caressed my skin like the familiar touch of a lover.

Nora was waiting for me on the sofa. She had changed into a full-length white silk nightgown, with thin shoulder straps and a front side slit that showed off a tantalizing glimpse of thigh. Her hair was unpinned now, too, trailing down her shoulders like tendrils of dark ivy. When Nora saw me her face lit up like the Christmas tree. She uncurled from the sofa and slowly walked across the thick white snowlike carpet to meet me. We stood in front of the Christmas tree admiring each other.

"The robe looks beautiful on you," Nora said. Her voice was low, breathy.

I blushed a little. "Thanks."

"There are other presents for you under the tree," Nora said. "But you have to wait until midnight to open those. Okay?"

"Whatever you want," I said.

"Mmmm. Right now, Holly, I want you," Nora said. She pulled me to her and kissed me again. But this wasn't the sort of soft, lingering kiss she had given me before. This was a hot kiss, hungry, her lips fierce against mine. She untied the sash around my waist without breaking the kiss and got the kimono open, sliding eager hands over my slender hips. I flicked my tongue over hers, teasing her. Nora answered with a soft moan, keeping one hand on my hip and sliding the other upward to cup my breast. She kneaded the supple flesh with the butt of her palm, using her thumb to stroke my nipple hard. It was my turn to moan.

Nora took us both to the floor. I didn't mind doing it there. The plush white carpet was soft and luxurious on my bare ass. Better than some beds I've fucked in. Nora was propped up on one side. She smiled down at me as she ran her bare foot up and down my leg. I reached up, tangled my fingers in her long, dark hair and pulled her mouth to mine. She didn't fight it. As we kissed again Nora's hands glided over my naked body, touching me as far as she could reach, sliding over my breasts, my thighs, my belly, then, finally, saving it for last, Nora brushed her fingers over my pussy. I moaned and arched against her, not because I thought that's what she wanted for her five hundred dollars but because I needed more, needed her to touch me there.

Keeping her hand between my legs, Nora slowly kissed her way down to my breast. She raked my hardened nipple with the very tip of her tongue, then took the firm nub into her mouth and sucked it, gently, her lips like crushed velvet. I writhed under Nora as she kissed one breast and then the other, wishing she would put her fingers inside me already. But she didn't. Nora stroked my cunt lips like she wasn't really thinking about it. Her attention was all on my breasts. She kissed and licked and sucked them until my nipples were almost painfully hard. When she grazed one with her teeth I whimpered softly. I felt her grin around my breast.

Nora plunged her fingers into me. I was wet enough to take them easily. She pumped in and out of me, fucking me hard and fast. I groaned and lifted my hips to meet her, humping her hand, a desperate, needy whore wanting it so bad I could have screamed. Nora started off with two fingers but worked up to three, thrusting deeper and deeper, taking me, owning me. Her rhythm was furious but steady. She knew how to fuck. I drew up my knees, spreading myself wider for her. Nora gave me four of her fingers, filling my pussy with them, pounding into me under the blinking lights of the Christmas tree. When she looked at me I knew she wasn't going to stop there. I didn't want her to. Something in my eyes must have told her so because Nora tucked her thumb under her fingers and in one final push was up to her wrist in my pussy.

I howled at the ceiling, grabbing fistfuls of carpet as Nora fucked me with her fist. She moved her hand in a slow, jerking motion, each movement sending giant waves of pleasure crashing over me. Heat flared in my cunt, then slowly crept up my body until every part of me felt like it was on fire. The blinking lights on the Christmas tree blurred into one and I felt dizzy, but it was a euphoric, giddy kind of dizzy that made me want to laugh and cry at the same time.

With her hand still inside me, Nora got her face between my legs and dragged her tongue over my swollen clit. It was like setting a match to gasoline. I came in a sudden, uncontrollable rush, my hips rising off the carpet as the orgasm surged through me. My pussy tightened around Nora's wrist and I cried out, a pitiful, choking sound caught somewhere deep in my throat. As the last tremors of climax rippled through me Nora flicked her tongue over my clit again, pulling her hand out of me with a sloppy wet plop. It set me off again. When I cried out this time it sounded remarkably like I was saying, "Nora."

Lips touched mine and brought me back from wherever I had been for those few magical moments. I stared up into Nora's eyes and just wanted to lose myself in them forever.

I rolled Nora onto her back. She surrendered her body to me with a breathless sigh, lazily tossing one arm over her head. Nora's nipples were thick and fat just like I had imagined them and they strained against the bosom of her nightgown. I lowered my mouth to her breast and sucked her nipple through white silk, stroking it off with my lips. Nora moaned softly, squirming on the carpet as I suckled at her breasts, each in turn, leaving two giant wet spots on her nightgown. She was breathing harder now and when she looked at me her eyes were glassy with desire.

"Eat me, please," Nora whispered.

I hiked up her nightgown. Nora had a neatly trimmed bush of dark hair framing her perfect cunt. The lips were pink and fleshy and shiny with arousal. Her clit was a glistening pearl at the center. I breathed in the musky scent of her, then pressed my mouth to her slit, sucking her pussy, licking up and down the length of her warm, wet furrow, then dipping inside. She groaned softly. Fingers tangled in my hair. Milky white thighs quivered on either side of my face as I lapped at Nora's meaty folds, fucking her with my tongue. Her sweet nectar flowed over my lips and I slurped it all up, every drop, wanting all of her, everything she would give me. I could feel her pussy spasm around me. She was so close. Pulling back her lips with my fingers, I exposed the shaft of her clit and flicked it with my tongue, lashing it, coaxing it out a little more until I could wrap my lips around it. Nora's grip in my hair tightened then her hips rose off the carpet. I wouldn't let go. Her moans echoed through the living room but I still kept at it, sucking on her clit until her body went limp and my face was drenched in her juices.

We lay there under the blinking lights of the Christmas tree, me draped across her belly, Nora running her fingers through my hair. I traced the wet spots on her nightgown with the tip of my finger. She purred with contentment.

"Will you stay until tomorrow?" Nora asked. "We can open presents in the morning and then I'll make us a nice Christmas dinner. I'll give you another five."

Even without the extra five I would have stayed, until tomorrow and longer. But Nora didn't need to know that. I wondered what kinds of presents she had for me, and what we would have for dinner. I nuzzled my face into her breast and whispered, "Sure."

Amanda and the Elf
Jean Roberta

It was Christmas Eve, and Amanda was exhausted. Finally, the house looked tidy enough for tomorrow's dinner guests. Enticingly wrapped presents for Jason and Jennifer nestled beneath the tree so that they wouldn't think Santa had forgotten them. "Psst!"

"Who's there?" asked Amanda. She suspected it might be her drunken ex-husband, overwhelmed with self-pity and a brief, seasonal attack of love for the children.

"It's me, baby." The voice was loud enough, and deep enough, but Amanda couldn't see where it was coming from.

"Duh," the voice persisted. "Look down, not up." Almost hidden behind the lower branches of the tree was a little man, about three feet tall, dressed in a tight green suit. He pulled off his stocking cap to reveal a head of messy red hair.

Amanda was tickled. "Aww. How did you get in here, little man?" She couldn't help thinking that all men should be that lightweight, harmless, and cute.

"I have my ways," he smirked. "You have no idea what I can do, Amanda. I work for the fat man himself, you know. I'm Puck the Elf. Rhymes with fuck."

The little man's expression reminded Amanda of the face of a horny boy in the throes of puberty, full of energy and mischief. Something about him seemed familiar. "Have we ever met before?"

A man-sized guffaw burst out of Puck like a cork from a bottle. "Remember when you were thirteen? Someone told you about candles and the necks of pop bottles, so you tried them? I loved watching you. You couldn't wait to get it from a real guy."

Amanda turned bright red. "Yeah, well," she remarked. "There's a saying: be careful what you wish for." She found the little man strangely attractive, and wished her desires were more logical. "That was a long time ago," she reminded him. "Why are you here now?"

He grinned. "I'm your present, babe. You've been working hard all year. The big guy notices these things, and you made it to his Good Girl list. He sent me to play with you. I signed up for it."

Amanda, who really did love children (when they were not throwing tantrums) sat on the sofa and gestured for him to sit on her lap. He swaggered closer and flexed a little arm until a hard bicep popped up on it like a hazelnut.

"Wanta see?" he offered. He unzipped his pants (which, on closer inspection, looked like deerskin) to reveal a tightly rolled organ that looked like a wet red tongue. It unrolled to a length of about nine inches and touched Amanda's lips.

They were open, as though to make a sound.

"Ohh," she sighed. The little man tore the clothes off his arms and legs and stood before her with the light bouncing off the muscles of his chest. His skin glowed, and he smelled like warm cinnamon.

"Remember now?" he asked her softly. He answered her unspoken invitation by hopping onto her lap. His muscular butt pressed comfortingly into her thighs. He was heavier than he looked.

Amanda held him in place, and her blonde hair hung around him like a veil. Tears welled up in her eyes, and she tried to blink them away. With some surprise, she realized how much she had missed him. "I didn't think you were real," she admitted. "I didn't think I'd ever see you again."

Puck looked smug. "Hello, 'Manda, who kicked me to the curb? You got a real boyfriend and said you didn't need me anymore. How was it, by the way?"

"Teenage romance is overrated," she complained. "And marriage is worse." She pushed him off her lap and stood, raising her crotch to his eye level. "I grew up," she told him. "I have some things to show you, too." She unbuttoned her blouse and wiggled out of her jeans. As he licked his lips, she unhooked her bra and threw it aside, then slid her panties down her legs. Her skin was pearly pink, and her light-brown bush was thicker and curlier than he remembered.

Two small, hard hands reached for the hair between Amanda's legs, which already glistened with moisture. Two fingers neatly grasped a sensitive button of flesh and rolled it, making it swell. More fingers slid into a wet tunnel. Amanda sank to her knees and closed her eyes.

"No, watch," he told her. "And if you don't make enough noise, I'll stop." His mouth closed around one of her stiff pink nipples. A tongue to match the organ lower down flicked and licked her, and a set of sharp teeth nibbled her.

"The kids will wake up," gasped the woman.

Puck pulled on her nipples until they were twice their usual size. He left them wet. "No, they won't," he assured her. "I sprinkled them with Elf Powder Number 24, so they'll sleep until you've had your second cup of morning coffee. It won't hurt them. You can scream as loud as they do."

"But can you—will this—?" she asked anxiously.

"Naw," grinned her eager suitor. "I can't give you an elf baby. Interspecies reproduction doesn't work, no matter what the ancient Greeks thought. You ever seen a centaur? Or a human bitch with puppies? Ever wonder why not?"

Amanda felt reassured, since her life was already complicated enough. She stretched herself out on her newly vacuumed carpet, feeling the prickly acrylic fibers against her back. She spread her legs. The little man lay on her, pressing his head against her beating heart.

Puck's long, flexible organ sank into her hot cunt until it filled her completely. Amanda encouraged him with pushes and squeezes as his organ changed shape and size to stroke every fold and crevice. She moaned and squealed until she popped like a Christmas cracker. Puck seemed happy to oblige her, which seemed only natural. It was his mission.

"You come faster than you used to," Puck remarked, his head between her breasts. She could feel the vibrations of his surprisingly manly voice, as though he were actually strumming her heart like a musical instrument.

"More practice," she answered. "Less time."

"Do you want more pressure?" pondered the little man. His organ seemed to grow as hard as rock and sprout little nubs or fingers that scratched Amanda's inner walls.

"Ohh," she moaned. "Not yet, Puck."

"Too much for you?" he bragged. "Baby, you're really tight for a mother of two. I want to stretch you out a bit before the night is over."

"They do Caesareans a lot these days," the woman informed him. "And you didn't even notice the scars. Could you stretch me little by little? I want to feel, you, Puck. I want to remember you later. But I mean, you know, there are limits."

"Sure, babe," he purred. "Anything you want. Just ask me. I might make you beg, but whatever you want you'll get, and get, and get." The elf's organ, still longer and thicker than that of Amanda's ex-husband (as she couldn't help noticing) pumped steadily into her very wet and sensitive pussy.

As the woman's breathing speeded up, a long, sly, elfin finger slid under her. "Do you still like it in the ass?" he asked. This question alone almost sent her over the edge.

"Uh, I—" gasped Amanda.

"That means yes," chuckled her little suitor. His finger, slippery with some kind of magical coating, slid into her anus and continued pushing deeper and deeper. Amanda turned red as her muscles automatically squeezed to discourage the invader. The resulting tingles seemed to rush immediately into her clit.

"Oh!" exhaled the tormented woman.

Puck shivered all over with the satisfaction of a job well done. "Louder, girl," he prompted. "Come on, I want to hear you."

With all the intensity of a woman whose voice has been silenced for years, Amanda howled like a wolf and wailed like a banshee. She sang, cooed, hummed, and growled as her companion pushed her, teased her, dared her, and praised her.

When Puck told her to lie facedown on a cushion from the sofa, Amanda arranged herself in the desired position with a self-conscious wiggle, looking back at the elf who was studying her ivory asscheeks as though wondering what sort of attention they needed. The first slap of his hard little hand brought the blood to her skin and a sigh to her lips, but she didn't object. "Oh yes," she remarked. He spanked her so well that she knew she would remember him while sitting at her dining room table for Christmas dinner.

Amanda vaguely wondered whether the little man who had volunteered to please her might be pleasing himself by paying her back for her long neglect. If so, she thought philosophically, so be it. She hadn't realized before how much a mother could need a spanking.

The dry heat in Amanda's firm behind (of which she was still vain) was soothed by long, wet strokes of Puck's hot tongue, which found its way between her legs to her excited clit. This time, Amanda was really alarmed by her extreme reactions to his touch, and asked him to stop. Puck was not convinced of her sincerity, so he held her in place until her next explosion brought her a few moments of sweet relief.

By the time Christmas morning spread its pale yellow light over the eastern horizon, Amanda had been fucked in all her openings, including both ears. She had been on her back, on her hands and knees, and curled spoon-fashion on her side. She had tasted Puck's peppermint-flavored cum.

Amanda's movements became as languid as those of an underwater swimmer. Her eyelids flickered and drooped.

The elf remained as bouncy and springy as ever. "Merry Christmas, baby," he crooned in her ear.

"Merry Christmas, little stud," she snickered back. She

yawned. "I need to sleep. My parents will be coming over for turkey dinner."

Puck pulled a stray strand of tinsel out of her hair. The charm of toys and magical beings tickled her to the core, but her mortal limitations could not be ignored. He was not of her world.

He seemed to read her mind. "I'll be back next year," he grinned. "If you're good."

"If I'm here," she promised. "Puck, my man," she sighed, "reality is hard to ignore, and I can't promise to wait for you." She crawled off to her bed, where she sank into dreams of cranberry sauce on torn wrapping paper and miniature boot-prints on new-fallen snow. She'd had enough satisfaction to give her sweet dreams for all twelve nights of an old-fashioned Christmas.

Trimming the Tree
Alex Mendra

"Open it." His voice was low, demanding.

Of course, that was the problem, or should I say, the challenge. Paul and I love Christmas: the great food, the giving of gifts, and the traditions. We always open one gift each on Christmas Eve. This year, the moment he walked in from work, he chose the biggest one under the tree, a telescope I bought him so we could spy on that sexy couple that lives in the apartment across the courtyard. They like to play in front of their window. I wanted us to have a better view.

This seemed to set him off: without so much as putting his eye to the telescope, he threw me onto the living room floor and fucked me. We didn't make love. He hiked my dress up, pulled my panties down, and fucked me, hard and simple. He finished by pulling his cock out of me and pumping it with his right hand, shooting all over my face and dress.

We didn't say a word. We fucked like strangers, and it made me hot. After, I stood up and took the dress off, thinking I'd pop into the shower for a quick rinse, and maybe some alone time with the shower massager.

Then, as soon as I was naked, he was on me again, pinning me to the carpet, facedown, hands behind my back. I felt the cold steel clasping around my wrists, heard the clicking whir of handcuffs binding me. Rolling onto my side, I watched as he slid effortlessly out of his suit pants and shirt. Seeing him stripped down to nothing, I could tell by his semierect cock that he still had some holiday tension to release.

"Tough day at the office?" I tried say, but it only sounded like a faint, nervous whisper. I wanted more, and he knew it, feeding on that knowledge.

This was the moment he chose to pick out a gift for me to open. All the lights in the room were off, except for the low glow of the tree, that yule light casting eerie shadows throughout the room. Kneeling beside me, his member inches from my lips, he placed a small, brown box on the floor. A thin red ribbon was tied around it in a bow. It was my turn. But with a catch.

"Use your mouth," he commanded.

I wasn't sure if he meant for me to use it on the box or the cock. Naturally, I chose the cock, craning my neck, sucking it in, still semisoft. Murmuring something under his breath about my lack of sexual morals, Paul pushed me off of my side, onto my back. He literally mounted my mouth, began thrusting, and was rigid in seconds.

I could hardly breathe, trying to snatch bits of air through my nose while his cock slid out of my throat and his en-gorged head slipped across the roof of my watering mouth. The weight of my body was crushing my bound hands into the floor. Finally, he pulled his slick cock out, and straddled my face, kneeling.

"Suck my balls. Suck my fucking balls!" he growled, and thrust one of his fingers deep into my soaking cunt.

As soon as I had one of his giant orbs in my mouth, he pulled his well-lubricated finger out of my pussy and buried it in his own ass. Paul's hips were bucking wildly, rising up to meet his hand wrapped around his cock, and immediately falling back down to plunge his finger deeper. I sucked on the globe in my mouth harder than usual; I thought surely he'd make me ease up, that it might hurt too much. When I looked up, I saw he didn't care. Head tossed back, eyes half-slits of ecstasy, he continued to fuck his hand and his ass in a frenzy of blind lust, finally exploding all over my face.

"Look what you made me do," he croaked hoarsely.

"I'm sorry." I didn't mean it, and he knew I didn't.

"Open," he demanded, now standing over me, pointing to the small brown box.

Rolling back onto my side, I felt awkward and exposed, teetering unsteadily, my cunt swollen with desire.

"Spread your ass and open the box," Paul chanted.

With my bound hands, I did as he demanded, pulling my cheeks apart. He was behind me now, and he began massaging my tight opening with two fingers. My face flushed with heat, I was dizzy with excitement. Pinning the box down with my chin, I finally managed to undo the red ribbon and flip the lid off by using a combination of tongue and teeth. When I looked inside and saw my gift, my dizziness became downward spiral of fear and helpless desire.

The box held a pair of shiny silver pruning shears with red handles.

Not sure of their intended use, I almost came just looking

at them. I trusted Paul, and knew he was in love with me. I also knew this was going to hurt.

He reached over me, one hand still playing with my ass, and gently lifted the shears out of the box. Holding them inches from my eyes, he slid a finger inside of me as I took a good long look at their menacing blades. My body was practically convulsing around his finger, and I found myself trying to back down onto his hand, pushing it deeper. Paul opened the blades ever so slightly and raked the cold, cutting edge over my rock-hard nipple. A nipple that was hard-wired directly to my cunt. I was soaking my thighs, dripping all over the carpet.

"Time to pay for being so bad," he whispered in my ear.

In a flash his finger was out of me, and I found myself rolled onto my stomach, ass high in the air. He touched me there, just once, with the steel blade. Then I watched him stand up, his cock swollen, his face serious with a majestic purpose. Paul walked over to the tree, shears in hand, and clipped a thick branch from the bottom of the Douglas fir. Trimming the smaller branches from the main, he quickly customized it into a supple switch.

Then I knew that it didn't matter if I'd been naughty *or* nice.

When the Giving Got Good
M. Christian

"Hope you like it," Ophelia said, crossed-legged on their scratchy bulls-eye rug, a wide, sweet smile on her face. She was good at a lot of things, finding a parking space on even the most insanely crowded street, making a rum cake that would make the Pope cry, giggling at cartoons; but she wasn't that good at hiding her excitement, not when the perfect spot opened up right in front of her, not when she made a rum cake that actually made her cry, not on Saturday morning just before the *Powerpuff Girls*, and definitely not on Christmas morning.

"Well, I hope you like mine, too," Henri said, perched on the edge of her favorite chair, a simple blue rocker, fingers knitted together in elegant contemplation. She was good at a lot of things, too—singing an aria from *La Boheme*, expounding on Aboriginal culture, debugging Windows—but even she wasn't that good at hiding excitement. Not when she hit that note just right, not when she suddenly understood what the Dreamtime was really about, or when she got the damned thing to boot, and definitely not on Christmas morning.

"I know I will," Ophelia said, her tones musical, a wind chime caught in a warm breeze. In photos, she was the beaming one, the bright and shinning one. Hair the color of polished gold, cut into a precious bowl, Ophelia was a sprite, a faery, a nymph: marzipan and spun sugar. Something that should be dancing on the top of the tree.

"And I know that whatever you give me will be wonderful," said Henri, her voice low and rumbling, thunder and deep ocean waves. In photos, she was the dark one, a great mahogany Buddha. Hair kinked and curled, only a little blacker than her gleaming obsidian skin, Henri was strength, determination, caution, and concentration. She was a mighty oak, a stately sequoia.

In the nearby kitchen, stuck to the white, pebbled metal of the fridge by a magnet disguised as sashimi, surrounded by similarly magnetic letters spelling out elegant haiku (Henri) and girlish dirty words (Ophelia) was one photograph: the sprite with thin white arms around the black Buddha. Despite their differences, there was a commonality about them. In spite of their different ways of doing it (smiling) and being it (happy), they were doing it obviously with each other, together.

But there was just one picture on the fridge, a photograph of the two of them. Just one. And it wasn't that old: less than a year, no more than a few months.

"Our first Christmas together. I'm so excited!" Ophelia said, reaching for her clowns and balloons coffee mug for an experimental sip of still-too-hot-to-really-drink cocoa.

"I can tell, sweetness," Henri said, taking a bite of rum cake from the plate precariously balanced on the arm of her rocker. "And so am I."

"I can't wait for you to see what I got you. I'm sure you're going to love it."

"I'm sure I will. I just hope you like mine."

"Oh, I know it's going to be fabu," Ophelia giggled, stretching out to grab a big box wrapped with gold and silver stars, curly ribbons, and a miniature snow-frosted tree, from in front of their cold, unworking fireplace. " 'Cause it'll come from you!"

"Oh, you say that," Henri said, taking another bite of cake and moving the plate down to her feet, "but I don't want to disappoint you."

"You won't, silly!" Ophelia slid her big box over to her lover's sandaled feet, touching unpainted toes to wrapping paper. "Open! Open! Open!"

"Not yet, sweetness," purred Henri, bending down to retrieve a small brown box from where it had been carefully hidden under her chair. "This is for you."

"Oooooh," cooed Ophelia, accepting it with reverence, but then shaking it once, good and hard, next to her tiny ears, listening for any incriminating sounds. "I can't wait!"

Henri laughed, a bass drum in the small room, the sound rolling off the walls. "It's a little something, but I hope it shows how much I care for you."

The sprite looked sad with joy for a moment, but the face wouldn't hold against her animated features. When it collapsed with a wide grin she bent down, picked up the big box and presented it to Henri. "Ditto! Let's open them together."

"Okay, that'll be fun." Henri's voice was softer than

usual, hushed by nerves. "I just hope you didn't spend that much. You know we don't have a lot of money."

"I know, I know—but it's Christmas, and Christmas is about giving and getting stuff. Can't have Christmas without giving and getting, right?"

"You're right. You're absolutely right, sweetness." Now her great voice was a low squeak. She surreptitiously wiped the back of her right hand under her eyes, hoping that the other girl didn't notice.

"Besides, silly, it didn't cost me anything! Not that you're not worth a lot, I mean."

Ophelia laughed, a bit deeper, a bit more assured. "I know what you mean. That's what I did with your gift as well. But you're priceless."

"Oh, silly!" Ophelia continued to rattle the box, trying to decipher the contents. "I was in the Community Exchange just the other day when I saw it. Your present, I mean. It leaped right out at me, saying, 'I'm just the right thing for Henri! Take me! Take me!' You know me, I can never say no to just the right thing." She stopped rattling and scooted over to rest her head against the big woman's thigh.

Henri stroked her blonde hair. "You are a precious girl, sweetness," she said, voice cracking yet again. She juggled her own present. "It is awfully heavy. I wonder what it could be?"

"Open! Open! Open!" chirped Ophelia, lifting her head and smiling. "I can't wait."

"Do yours, too. Come on, we'll open them together. Funny that you mention the Exchange, because that's where I got yours. Mary even said that it was the perfect present for you."

"That's so funny, Mary said the same about yours as well.

She is such a sweetheart, isn't she?"

"One of the best things in this world, I think. Right up there with you, sweetness." Tape popped, stretched until it broke over her finger. A bit of cardboard under the wrapping was revealed.

"Oh, you!" Ophelia giggled, while she worked the top off her box.

Paper rustled, some tore; cotton was lifted aside. During, dark eyes glanced over at blue, blue back at dark, watching each other watching each other, hoping for flashes of excitement and happiness, praying against disappointment.

Ophelia first, Henri handicapped by colorful wrapping paper. She held it up in front of her eyes: tiny, silver, and elegant, the soft music it made in their tiny room was clear and sharp. "It's a bell!" giggled Ophelia, chiming it gently with a rose and gold colored nail. "It's beautiful!"

"It's for your nipple ring," Henri said, bending down to be closer. "So you can wear it always, and so every time it rings you can remember me."

The sprite sniffled. "Oh, oh, oh," she said, unable to continue. "It's really lovely. Really, it's just that, well, I don't have my ring anymore, Henri. I'm so sorry! I traded it for…for what I got you."

Henri was dumb. She looked at the tiny silver chime, listened to the single clear note it still gently played between Ophelia's fingers. "Oh, sweetness, I didn't know."

"It's okay. It's okay, it really is. I'll keep it in my pocket. I'll put it on a string around my neck. It's wonderful, so special," she sniffled, loud and long, then looked embarrassed. "I'm sorry," she said, not really understanding why she said it. "Now you open yours. Open it! I'm sure you'll love it."

"Okay," the numb Henri said. Papers peeled completely away, revealing a box. The box was opened, revealing newspapers. Newspapers were pulled out showing something dark and wooden.

Henri held it up. "It's, it's—" she started to say, but didn't finish.

"It's a rack! A whip rack! Won't it be perfect for your flogger? You know, your favorite Jay Marsten toy? Won't it look wonderful?"

"My flogger? Oh, dear…sweetness…."

"Don't you like it? I thought it was just right for you. Isn't it?"

"I think it's wonderful. Really, it's perfect. It's just that, well, sweetness, I don't have the flogger anymore. I traded it in…for your bell."

Ophelia looked at Henri. Henri did the same back at Ophelia. The air grew clear, fragile, like it was going to shatter with tension.

Then Henri bellowed with delight, a great explosion of happiness, and dropped down off her chair to grab the little blonde sprite. Then Ophelia shrieked with joy, and rose to wrap her arms around the big black Buddha while they both laughed and cried, cried and laughed, until they fell over into a black and white, black and white tumble on the rug.

"My sweetness," Henri said, between long, soulful and quick, innocent kisses, her big arms wrapped around thin, little Ophelia.

"No," said Ophelia, dreamy grin on her face, "you're the sweet one. Sweet as anything. As sugar," a kiss on Henri's nose, "as honey," another kiss, same nose, "as frosting on a big piece of cake," another kiss—much longer, much deeper, lips to lips. After a long, slow time, it broke, and Ophelia finished her list with "as love."

Henri smiled, reaching down to lift the thin girl's T-shirt, exposing a buttery expanse of soft tummy. *"Au contraire,"* she said, lifting her head just long enough to playfully wag a finger, "you are the one who is sugar, honey, and frosting. All the good and precious stuff in this world is right here." Back to her rise of belly, a kiss to the silken skin.

"Oh," Ophelia said, voice tender and slightly lost.

"—and right here, of course." Ophelia had started the day in her T-shirt, still on, though pushed up, and comfy, slightly threadbare sweatpants. But not for long. Dark fingers slipped between skin and pants, Henri gently tugged, persistently tugged, and then, when they were down to her ankles, pulled them off—and tossed them into a far corner without a further thought.

"Oh," Ophelia said, voice even more tender, even more lost.

Hands on her thighs, with very little insistence, Henri parted her legs. Eyes wide with glee, and more than a little wonder, she stopped to look, to simply look. After a time she said, repeating but meaning more: "All that's precious and good in the world. Well, my world, at any rate. I could just eat you up."

Another kiss, different set of lips: Henri to Ophelia. Fingers gently stroking down, touching the smaller girl's outer lips, then holding them, pulling just enough to part. Again, a look, a watch, an admiration, before that kiss. After the kiss, lips to clit this time, Henri to Ophelia, another kiss. But then it was more than a kiss, or just a different form of a kiss: lips and tongue, stroking, flicking, washing, following the lifts and tucks, the silken contours of her. In response, Ophelia cooed and purred, a great blonde kitty, and spread her legs a bit more.

No time. Nothing in the world but Henri, kneeling down, lips and tongue, then fingers, playing her lover, playing with her lover. It really wasn't a goal, per se, but it happened anyway: Ophelia's breathing quickened, her thighs tensed, her fingers gripped the rug in itch-filled fists, and then it came out, hissed and screamed out of her.

"Sweet, deliciously sweet—" cooed Henri, running her fingers up and down Ophelia's thighs, tactile applause. "I could just eat you up, nibble on you all day."

"Whew!" the thin blonde girl said, springing up—elbows on the rug, propping herself up. A thin strand of gold hair lazily dripped down her forehead. "I do exclaim, I do: whew!"

Henri didn't say anything. She just traced slow, lazy circles on Ophelia's tummy and smiled.

"—and as for who's the tasty one!" Quick, giggling like a maniac, hands suddenly on Henri's wide shoulders, pushing, toppling the bigger woman back. Tangled, this time it was Ophelia on top, Ophelia's hands that were tugging at clothing, revealing the other woman's mountainous black breasts and even darker, already hardening nipples.

"Oh, no, oh, no, oh, no, oh, no, oh, no, oh, no, oh, no, oh, no…," Henri said, eyes wide, mouth open. "You're not going to—"

"I most certainly am," Ophelia said, her words slurred, her teeth cleanly locked around Henri's nipple. "Asfolutery, ah am."

"Oh, no, oh, no, oh, no, oh, no," Henri said, her deep voice breaking, straining as the spill of denial flowed from her mouth.

"Ready?" the other girl said, delight and mischief winking in her pale blue eyes.

"Oh, no—" Henri started, but didn't finish. The next words—probably "Oh, no—" were cut off, washed away by a sharp, long hiss as Ophelia's teeth carefully, methodically, bit down on her swollen nipple.

The squeeze was consummate, the control expert. Pearly whites like exact tools, perfect clamps. Slowly, glacially, Ophelia bit down just a bit more, anywhere else on the body unnoticeable—on Henri's fat, erect nipple, it was like a steel trap teasing at one of her most sensitive points.

Again, a bit more force, again the low hiss like steam that whistled out from between Henri's lips, but this time there was something more: a flick, a touch of warm wetness as Ophelia's tongue touched, then grazed, then stroked at the very tip.

The teeth went on, squeezing down harder and harder, the tongue went on, licking, adding something subtle and sweet to the ferocious bite. Sometimes, Henri would come this way, just from Ophelia's precise nibbles to her breasts and nipples. But sometimes she needed, or just wanted, something more.

Still leaning back, she freed one arm, turning herself so she wouldn't lose balance, and grabbed hold of Ophelia's left arm. At the touch, the other woman allowed herself to be led, hand grazing the front of Henri's jeans. "Rub me...please," Henri managed to hiss out, the fear of having to move with Ophelia's teeth still locked around her nipple almost pushing her over the edge.

Ophelia smiled, never once releasing her grip, and with that guided arm, she undid Henri's belt, unbuttoned her fly, and snaked her hand down between her thighs.

Warm, at first, then hot. Humid, at first, then steamy—then wet as Ophelia's fingers deftly slipped between her lover's great thighs. There, down among slippery lips, she found what she was looking for, what both of them were hoping for: a hard kernel, a very firm clit.

Lips and teeth tight and relentless, tongue magically adding to it all, Ophelia rubbed Henri's clit, building it all up, pushing her lover up higher and higher—until there was nowhere else to go.

Henri's version was a bellow, a roar, a scream that tensed and released through the whole body. Even one of her legs was sucked into the wonderful release: it kicked and jerked in perfect tune with her heavy breaths, the beat of her moans and sighs.

She collapsed, falling back onto the rug, arms out at her sides, legs recklessly apart. On top, snuggling up to her breasts, curling around her thighs, Ophelia curved and folded herself so that as much of her as possible was touching the other woman, and that way they both faded, drifted off, and slept, dreaming of sugar, sweetness, heat, steam, and, of course, each other.

Sometime later, one woke—with the other following right after. Grinning as they stumbled, they got drinks, went to the bathroom, but mostly just stood in the middle of their tiny apartment and kissed: lips to lips, black to white, big to small, love and love.

A few minutes later, after some relief and sips of water, they decided to take a little walk, to enjoy something amazing and absolutely free: the sights and sounds of their nice neighborhood, their lovely city.

When they opened the door they saw the box. Wrapped

in pretty, and somewhat familiar, paper: gold stars, pale blue. Very pretty.

Puzzling, they took it inside, tore and peeled back the paper, opened the box. Inside were two simple, but very special, things: a lovely leather flogger and a tiny silver ring—just perfect for a nipple.

There was also a card.

> *Merry Christmas, my lovely friends. I hope you like what I gave you. Never forget that presents are just things, and that love, and who you love, are the most special gifts anyone can give and get in this world.*

The card was from the Community Exchange, and the signature read:

Love, Mary.

Christmas Past
Alison Tyler

Flash back to Christmas 1987. My first trip home from college. The prospect of coming home was exciting. Actually *being* home turned out to be far less so. After only a few minutes trapped indoors, I couldn't wait to get out of the house, away from the smells of overcooked goose and sickly-sweet pecan pie, and far, far away from my childhood bedroom and childhood memories.

I had plans to catch up with friends over the next few days, but this first evening home was supposed to be reserved for family time. And so I bolted. In the pale twilight, I wandered alone along University Avenue, mentally criticizing the town where I'd grown up. Colored leaves fluttered along the sidewalk and small white Christmas lights twinkled in the barren trees, but I couldn't see the charm. The scenario was all too Norman Rockwell for me, when Francis Bacon would have more aptly suited my mood. Where was a *Screaming Pope* when you needed one?

As I strolled down the streets, I became keenly aware that everything about my hometown looked smaller than it had three months before. The Varsity movie theater. The Creamery. The streets themselves. I felt old. Done with this part of my world. No more childhood. No more fucking around. Nothing was the same.

At least, not until I saw Matt.

Flash back to Christmas vacation 1984. The Varsity Theater. The place seemed big then, bigger than anything with its cavernous two-tiered balcony and the smell of decades of popcorn and spilled soda pop. At the midnight screening of *The Rocky Horror Picture Show*, Matt sat with his arm around me in the very last row. I remember warmth and the smell of his skin and the worn crimson velvet seats. I sported vibrant blue streaks in my dark hair, and for this date—our first—I wore shiny Doc Martins that matched that cobalt hue. The boots were heavier than concrete blocks, and had taken me a summer's worth of babysitting hours to earn, but I worshipped them. They made me feel cool and in control. I hadn't known shoes could do that before.

The truth was that I was neither cool nor in control. I had a wild crush on this high school athlete, and I didn't have any idea how to deal with that. He was older than me by two years, and he liked me. I could feel how much he liked me. The night was perfect, down to the flavor of Sweet Tarts on my tongue when we kissed goodnight. And that's how far I let it go.

Now, I sat on the concrete ledge in front of the Varsity wearing faded jeans and a long-sleeved gray sweater. My hair was longer and my face thinner than in my high school days. I wasn't sporting punk streaks anymore, but I did have on my latest Docs, glistening patent leather black ones purchased at a hip store on the ever-trendy Melrose Avenue.

As if approaching out of a dream, Matt, a college junior, walked toward me in the purple-tinted twilight and gave me a huge bear hug. I felt as if I were disappearing into him. He stood between my spread legs holding me tight, and he pressed his lips to my hair and whispered, "I missed you, Jodie."

"How'd you know I would be here?"

"It's our place," he smiled. With his words, everything magically became the right size again. I didn't feel as if I were caught "Twilight Zone"-style in a minuscule town made up of tiny insignificant streets, waiting for a giant hand to scoop me out. Everything felt perfectly proportionate as Matt lifted me off the concrete ledge and then led me through the courtyard of the Varsity to the graffiti-sprayed alley behind. This was a shortcut to the parking lot, a place where smokers used to hang out. Now, on the holiday eve, it was empty.

Matt pushed me up against the painted wall and we made out. Fiercely. Sweetly. Or should I say bittersweetly? Because with Matt that's all it could be. In two weeks, we would be heading back to our respective schools. Back to the other flirtations in our other lives. But with his hand in my long soft hair and his warm lips on mine, I lost it all. The jaded quality that comes with being nineteen. The Doc Martin stomp. The permanent scowl. The angry flick of my hair whenever my mother tried to brush my long bangs out of my eyes. ("Your face is so pretty. Why do you have to hide it?")

With Matt in the alley behind the Varsity, I felt whole,

as I had whenever I was with him. Except this was different. We were borderline grown-ups now. We could vote. We could do the things I hadn't done in high school, but I had done in college. (Christ, the *real* things you learn in college.)

Everything had to go fast then. As if we couldn't wait to connect. He unbuttoned his 501s while I got out of my Docs, then slid my boot-cut jeans down past my slender thighs. He worked on the condom with finesse, then easily picked me up in his huge, muscular embrace. I held on to him with my legs around his waist as he slipped me back down onto his erection. I stared into his beautiful green eyes as I felt him inside me. *Really* inside of me. I gripped on to his strong arms, and moved my lithe body on his.

"God, I missed you," he said, his voice low.

"Yeah."

"Really, Jodie. Really."

"Yeah—" I said again, staring at him. And even as we were fucking in the alley behind the movie theater, my mind was elsewhere—slipping back in time, thinking about high school, remembering how I'd wanted to do this before, how he'd wanted me to, but how we never had. And now that we were, I understood somehow that it wasn't a big deal. It would have been before. But it wasn't going to be now.

Still, I wouldn't have traded that moment for anything. The way the cold air kissed my naked skin. (It can get cold in December—even in California.) The way his eyes never left mine as he fucked me. I held tightly to him. I pressed my body as firmly as I could to his, gaining that magic connection of skin on skin.

He knew exactly what to do. He moved me slowly, rhythmically, and I could feel the pleasure building gradually within me. He bounced me up and down until I felt myself getting closer to climax. The pleasure of our tight embrace pulsed through me, and my whole body shivered with anticipation. Then he set me down on the ground, my bare feet cold on the cracked and worn concrete, and he gruffly told me to turn away from him. I liked the rough command in his voice. He was a man now, not a boy, and I wondered what would happen if I didn't obey him, but I was too turned on to find out.

Quickly, I faced the alley, put my palms up against the concrete on a picture of the Rolling Stones' logo done in blood-red spray paint. I arched my back, letting him know that I was ready for him to enter me from behind. He slid in with ease, my body welcoming him with a series of frantic contractions. His cock felt so perfect inside me, and he thrust at the pace I needed, in and out and hard. So fucking hard.

I could hardly breathe from how good this felt. He drove inside of me, and with each thrust, I sucked in my breath in a shuddering gasp. My eyes were wide open, staring at the splashes of decades' old graffiti in front of me. But in my head, pictures blossomed that I couldn't stop. What had I done since I'd last seem him? Slept with a handsome drunk guy at a frat party. Fucked a classmate in his upper bunk bed while his roommate snored below us. Been sweetly fondled by two male ROTC friends while doing tequila shots after midterms. I was so much older now. I was ready for him.

He used one hand on my clit as he stroked me from behind. With his warm fingers, he skated up and down over my slippery clit, then used his thumb to press right on that hot button as he began to thrust harder, faster. Soon I was coming. Coming in the alley, coming a moment before he did and sighing as he called out my name.

Flash forward to now, more than fifteen years later, Christmas Eve once again. And there he is downtown. With his family. Two little ones and another on the way. There he is with his slight beer gut visible beneath his thick navy blue cable-knit sweater. There he is with his wife, her fragile blonde beauty that I remember from pictures of the wedding already fading, turning brittle at the edges. She has a no-nonsense haircut and a tired look in her steel gray eyes.

Matt rushes to greet me with that bear hug, a little too long this time. A little too tight. His wife is a beat behind him, but I feel her eyes focus on me as Matt tries to kiss me, a kiss on the cheek that doesn't quite meet my skin.

"You look the same—" he says, when he takes a step back, obviously ignoring the silver in my hair. Early silver, yes, but there just the same, replacing those rebellious blue streaks from high school twenty years ago. "Just the same."

But nothing's the same. The Varsity is a Borders Bookstore. The graffiti-decorated alley is painted over, clean and beige. Why is beige better? How can it possibly be?

"Really," he says, tilting his head at me, regarding me with those deep green eyes I used to dream about during science class. "So slim—" eyeing me up and down in my faded jeans, and my long-sleeved sweater, the same rainstorm gray shade as before, but this one is cashmere. I don't thrift-store shop as often as I used to. I can't hang out in the places where the teenagers go without feeling like the odd man out. Truth be told, I am far more secure in this Borders than I would be if it were the same old Varsity Theater that used to serve alcohol to underage teenage drinkers.

I see him choosing to dismiss the fine lines around my dark brown eyes and focus instead on the image that he remembers of me: the hot young chicklet in the back row of the movie theater. Was that twenty years ago? Can I be this old for real?

I wonder if he remembers our tryst in the alley. The rush of it. The necessary quality. We *had* to have that time together. We owed it to ourselves. Does he think about it every Christmas Eve, as he wraps the presents, as he carves the bird? No matter where he is, or whose family he's with, does the scent of gingery pie and crisp wintry air make him think of me?

Then his wife, pulled forward by two kids—and one on the way—calls over her shoulder in a tone of finality, "Nice to see you again. Merry Christmas, Josie—"

Quickly, Matt corrects her. "*Jodie*. She means Jodie. She's distracted, you know…."

And I shrug as he looks over his shoulder and sees she's busy corralling the little ones before he leans back down for one more kiss. A real one this time, not an air one or a cheek one. A real one, just like all those kisses before, hot and wet, and filled with that same passion from so many years ago.

But this one…this one is bittersweet.

About the Authors

Xavier Acton's writing has appeared previously in *Good Vibrations* magazine as well as in Gothic.net, Necromantic.com, the *Sweet Life* series, and the *Naughty Stories from A to Z* series.

Rachel Kramer Bussel (www.rachelkramerbussel.com) is senior editor at *Penthouse Variations*, a contributing editor at *Penthouse,* and writes the "Lusty Lady" column in the *Village Voice.* She is the editor of *Naughty Spanking Stories from A to Z* and *Cheeky: Essays on Spanking and Being Spanked,* and coeditor of *Up All Night: Adventures in Lesbian Sex,* with several more dirty books on the way. Her writing has been published in over sixty erotic anthologies, including *Best American Erotica 2004,* as well as publications such as *AVN, Bust, Curve, Diva, Girlfriends,* Gothamist.com, *On Our Backs,*

Oxygen.com, *Penthouse, Punk Planet, Rockrgrl,* the *San Francisco Chronicle,* and *Velvetpark.*

M. Christian is the author of the critically acclaimed and best-selling collections *Dirty Words, Speaking Parts,* and *The Bachelor Machine.* He is the editor of *The Burning Pen, Guilty Pleasures,* the *Best S/M Erotica* series, *The Mammoth Book of Future Cops* and *The Mammoth Book of Tales of the Road* (both with Maxim Jakubowski), and over fourteen other anthologies. His short fiction has appeared in over one hundred and fifty books including *Best American Erotica, Best Gay Erotica, Best Lesbian Erotica, Best Transgendered Erotica, Best Fetish Erotica, Best Bondage Erotica* and…well, you get the idea. He lives in San Francisco and is only some of what that implies.

Felix D'Angelo has written erotica for *Sweet Life 2, Best Bondage Erotica,* and *Good Vibrations* magazine. He currently lives in California with his very naughty girlfriend Katrina and their dog Anton.

Dante Davidson is a tenured professor in Santa Barbara, California. His short stories have appeared in *Bondage, Naughty Stories from A to Z, Best Bondage Erotica,* and *Sweet Life.* With Alison Tyler, he is the coauthor of the best-selling collection of short fiction *Bondage on a Budget* and *Secrets for Great Sex After Fifty* (which he wrote at age twenty-eight).

Simone Harlow is the pseudonym for a multi-published romance writer. She lives in a small Southern California town where the horses outnumber the people. The former Catholic schoolgirl believes that one can never own too many red lipsticks, that being a certain Irish actor's love slave would be a great gig, and that you should commit one naughty act daily. Her short stories have also appeared in *Heat Wave* and *Down & Dirty Volume 2*.

Michelle Houston has been writing erotica since 1995. She has five ebooks out from Renaissance E Books, as well as a print omnibus of two of them, and stories in several anthologies. Michelle lives in the eastern United States with her husband and daughter. You can read more about her, or see more of her writing on her personal website, The Erotic Pen (www.eroticpen.net). She loves to receive email, so drop her a line at thewriter@eroticpen.net.

Lynne Jamneck's fiction and nonfiction have appeared in various publications including *Best Lesbian Erotica 2003*, *Heat Wave*, *Best of On Our Backs Volume 2*, *Naked Erotica*, *H. P. Lovecraft's Magazine of Horror*, *Raging Horrormones,* and *Ultimate Lesbian Erotica 2005*. Her first mystery, *Down the Rabbit Hole* (a Samantha Skellar mystery) is available from Bella Books. She is the creator and editor of *Simulacrum: The Magazine of Speculative Transformation*. (www.specficworld.com/simulacrum.html). She likes vodka over ice, antiheroes, and thinks *dyke* is the sexiest word in the dictionary. Email her at lynnejamneck@xtra.co.nz.

JT Langdon is the Buddhist, vegetarian, and lover of chocolate responsible for such novels as the *Lady Davenport's Slave* trilogy, *Sisters of Omega Pi, Hard Time,* and *For I Have Sinned*. Despite numerous requests to leave, some made with the pointy end of pitchforks, the author continues to live in the Midwest. Visit the author online at www.jtlangdon.com.

Molly Laster is a journalist who splits her time between Seattle and San Francisco, so she rarely gets a break from the weather! Her work has appeared in anthologies including *Girls on the Go*, *Naughty Fairy Tales from A to Z*, and *Naughty Stories from A to Z*.

Tsaurah Litzky has had stories appear in the *Best American Erotica* series (six times), as well as in *Politically Inspired*, *The Blacklisted Journalist*, *Williamsburg Observer*, The *Avant Porn Anthology*, *Naughty Spanking Stories from A to Z*, *Pink Pages*, and many other books and publications. Simon & Schuster published her novella, *The Motion of the Ocean*, in 2004 as part of the series of erotic novellas, *Susie Bright Presents: Three the Hard Way*. Tsaurah teaches erotic writing at the New School University. Her erotic writing class, Silk Sheets: Writing Erotica, was named Best Writing Class in New York City by the *Village Voice* in 2004.

Alex Mendra is a writer whose plays have been produced both in Europe and in the United States. He was first runner-up in the Jim Highsmith Playwright Competition and a semifinalist in the Julie Harris Playwright Competition. His poetry has been published in *Shampoo Poetry* and *In Other Words.* His short stories have appeared in *Naughty Stories from A to Z Volume 2*, *Velvet Heat*, and *Best Bondage Erotica*. Alex has aired several radio essays on the NPR affiliate station KQED-FM.

N. T. Morley is the author of more than a dozen published novels of dominance and submission, including *The Parlor*, *The Limousine*, *The Circle*, *The Nightclub*, *The Appointment*, and the trilogies *The Library*, *The Castle*, and *The Office*. Morley has also edited two anthologies, *MASTER* and *slave*.

Tom Piccirilli is the author of thirteen novels including *A Choir of Ill Children*, *November Mourns*, *Grave Men*, and *Coffin Blues*. He's published over one hundred and fifty stories in the horror, mystery, fantasy, and erotica genres. Learn more about his work at www.tompiccirilli.com.

Ayre Riley has written for *Down & Dirty, Naughty Stories from A to Z Volumes 3 & 4*, and *slave*. She currently resides in Hollywood, Florida.

Jean Roberta teaches first-year English courses at a Canadian prairie university and spends much time in her imagination. Her erotic fiction has been widely published; her fantasy stories have appeared in *Best Lesbian Erotica 2000*, *Closet Desire IV: Flights of Fantasy*, *Monsters, Trans Figures: Transfigured Erotica*, and on the website Ruthiesclub.com. Her rants and reviews appear in her column, "In My Jeans," on the website Bluefood.cc.

Thomas S. Roche's more than three hundred published short stories and three hundred published articles have appeared in a wide variety of magazines, anthologies, and websites. In addition, his ten published books include *His* and *Hers,* two books of erotica coauthored with Alison Tyler, as well as three volumes of the *Noirotica* series. He has recently taken up erotic photography, which he showcases at his website, www.skidroche.com. After a lucky thirteen years in San Francisco, he recently relocated to New Orleans.

Simon Sheppard is, like Jesus, Jewish. He (Simon, not Jesus) is the author of the books *Sex Parties 101, In Deep: Erotic Stories,* and *Kinkorama: Dispatches from the Front Lines* *of Perversion.* His work has appeared in over one hundred and twenty five anthologies, including many editions of *Best American Erotica* and *Best Gay Erotica,* and he writes the columns "Sex Talk" and "Perv." When he's not at work on a historically based anthology of gay porn, he loiters at www.simonsheppard.com.

Saskia Walker is a British author who has had short erotic fiction published on both sides of the pond. You can find her work in *Seductions: Tales of Erotic Persuasion, Sugar and Spice, More Wicked Words, Wicked Words 5 & 8, Naughty Stories from A to Z Volume 3, Naked Erotica, Taboo, Three-Way,* and *Sextopia.* She also writes erotic romance for Red Sage Publishing. Her first novella, *Summer Lightning,* will be available soon. Visit www.saskiawalker.co.uk.

Eric Williams has written for anthologies including *Sweet Life* and *Naughty Stories from A to Z Volume 3.*

About the Editor

Called "a trollop with a laptop" by *East Bay Express*, **Alison Tyler** is naughty and she knows it. Over the past decade, Ms. Tyler has written more than fifteen explicit novels including *Learning to Love It, Strictly Confidential, Sweet Thing, Sticky Fingers*, and *Something About Workmen* (all published by Black Lace), and *Rumors* (Cheek). Her novels have been translated into Japanese, Dutch, German, Norwegian, and Spanish. Her stories have appeared in anthologies including *Sweet Life 1 & 2; Taboo; Best Women's Erotica 2002, 2003 & 2005; Best of Best Women's Erotica; Best Fetish Erotica;* and *Best Lesbian Erotica 1996* (all published by Cleis); and in *Wicked Words 4, 5, 6, 8 & 10; Sex at the Office* and *Sex on Holiday* (Black Lace); as well as in *Playgirl* magazine. She is the editor of *Batteries Not Included* (Diva); *Heat Wave, Best Bondage Erotica 1 & 2*, and *Three-Way* (all from Cleis Press); *Naughty Fairy Tales from A* *to Z* (Plume); and the *Naughty Stories from A to Z* series, the *Down & Dirty* series, *Naked Erotica*, and *Juicy Erotica* (all from Pretty Things Press). Please visit www.prettythingspress.com.

Ms. Tyler knows that Santa doesn't have to check his list twice to discover that she's been naughty, naughty, naughty. And she wishes Joy to the World to everyone. (To make a *Joy to the World*, pour 1 1/2 oz. light rum, 1/2 oz. bourbon, and 1/2 oz. dark crème de cacao into a mixing glass nearly filled with ice. Stir. Strain into a cocktail glass. Cheers!)

I used to be Snow White, but I drifted.

—Mae West

More Bestselling Erotica from Alison Tyler

Best Bondage Erotica 2
Edited by Alison Tyler
One of the most prolific writers of erotica today, editor Alison Tyler has assembled a collection of playful and dangerously explicit stories that will grab you and never let you go.
ISBN 1-57344-214-3 $14.95

Best Bondage Erotica
Edited by Alison Tyler
ISBN 1-57344-173-2 $14.95

Heat Wave
Sizzling Sex Stories
Edited by Alison Tyler
ISBN 1-57344-189-9 $14.95

Three-Way
Erotic Stories
Edited by Alison Tyler
ISBN 1-57344-193-7 $14.95

Bestselling Erotica for Couples

Expertly crafted, explicit stories about couples who try out their number one sexual fantasies—with explosive results. Sure to keep you up past bedtime.

Sweet Life
Erotic Fantasies for Couples
Edited by Violet Blue
Your ticket to a front row seat for first-time spankings, breathtaking role-playing scenes, sex parties, women who strap it on and men who love to take it, not to mention threesomes of every combination…
ISBN 1-57344-133-3 $14.95

Sweet Life 2
Erotic Fantasies for Couples
Edited by Violet Blue
ISBN 1-57344-167-8 $14.95

Taboo
Forbidden Fantasies for Couples
Edited by Violet Blue
ISBN 1-57344-186-4 $14.95
What is *your* deepest, darkest, sweetest, most stunningly wicked fantasy? *Taboo* will feed you erotic stories of forbidden desire like fingerfuls of warm chocolate dripping onto your tongue. Superbly written erotic stories featuring couples who want it so bad they can taste it—and they do, making their most taboo erotic fantasies come true.

Bestselling Erotica for Adventurous Readers

"My favorite neo-Victorian erotic romance writer...bring on the ponies!" —Susie Bright

AN EROTIC SM NOVEL

Molly Weatherfield

Carrie's Story
An Erotic S/M Novel
Molly Weatherfield
ISBN 1-57344-156-2 $12.95

"I had been Jonathan's slave for about a year when he told me he wanted to sell me at an auction. I wasn't in any condition to respond when he told me this..." So begins Carrie's tale of uncompromising sexual adventure. Imagine the *Story of O* starring a Berkeley PhD (who moonlights as a bike messenger) with a penchant for irony, self-analysis, and anal sex. Set in San Francisco and the Napa Valley, *Carrie's Story* takes the reader into the netherworld of slave auctions, training regimes, and human "ponies" preening for dressage competitions.

Safe Word
An Erotic S/M Novel
Molly Weatherfield
ISBN 1-57344-168-6 $12.95

The sequel to *Carrie's Story*. Whisked away to Greece, Carrie learns new, more rigorous methods of sexual satisfaction. When her year of training is complete, she faces a decision—life on her own or in the embrace of a beloved Master...

Boy in the Middle
Erotic Fiction
Patrick Califia
ISBN 1-57344-218-6 $14.95

Too Beautiful & Other Stories
Erotic Stories
Mark Pritchard
ISBN 1-57344-138-4 $14.95

How I Adore You
Erotic Stories
Mark Pritchard
ISBN 1-57344-129-5 $14.95

Best Erotica Series

"Gets racier every year."—*San Francisco Bay Guardian*

Buy 4 books, Get 1 FREE*

Best of Best Women's Erotica
Edited by Marcy Sheiner
ISBN 1-57344-211-9 $14.95

Best Women's Erotica 2006
Edited by Violet Blue
ISBN 1-57344-223-2 $14.95

Best Women's Erotica 2005
Edited by Marcy Sheiner
ISBN 1-57344-201-1 $14.95

Best Women's Erotica
Edited by Marcy Sheiner
ISBN 1-57344-099-X $14.95

Best Black Women's Erotica
Edited by Blanche Richardson
ISBN 1-57344-106-6 $14.95

Best Black Women's Erotica 2
Edited by Samiya Bashir
ISBN 1-57344-163-5 $14.95

Best Bisexual Women's Erotica
Edited by Cara Bruce
ISBN 1-57344-134-1 $14.95

Best Fetish Erotica
Edited by Cara Bruce
ISBN 1-57344-146-5 $14.95

Best of Best Lesbian Erotica 2
Edited by Tristan Taormino
ISBN: 1-57344-212-7 $14.95

Best of the Best Lesbian Erotica: 1996–2000
Edited by Tristan Taormino
ISBN 1-57344-105-8 $14.95

Best Lesbian Erotica 2006
Edited by Tristan Taormino; Selected and Introduced by Eileen Myles
ISBN 1-57344-224-0 $14.95

Best Lesbian Erotica 2005
Edited by Tristan Taormino; Selected and Introduced by Felice Newman
ISBN 1-57344-202-X $14.95

Best of Best Gay Erotica 2
Edited by Richard Labonté
ISBN 1-57344-213-5 $14.95

Best of the Best Gay Erotica: 1996–2000
Edited by Richard Labonté
ISBN 1-57344-104-X $14.95

Best Gay Erotica 2006
Edited by Richard Labonté; Selected and Introduced by Matt Bernstein Sycamore
ISBN 1-57344-225-9 $14.95

Erotic Fairy Tales
A Romp Through the Classics
Edited by Mitzi Szereto
ISBN 1-57344-124-4 $14.95

Hot Lesbian Erotica
Edited by Tristan Taormino
ISBN 1-57344-208-9 $14.95

Ordering is easy! Call us toll free to place your MC/VISA order or mail the order form below with payment to: Cleis Press, P.O. Box 14697, San Francisco, CA 94114.

ORDER FORM

Buy 4 books, Get 1 *FREE**

QTY	TITLE	PRICE
————	——————————————————————————	————
————	——————————————————————————	————
————	——————————————————————————	————
————	——————————————————————————	————
————	——————————————————————————	————
————	——————————————————————————	————
————	——————————————————————————	————
————	——————————————————————————	————
————	——————————————————————————	————
————	——————————————————————————	————
————	——————————————————————————	————

SUBTOTAL ————

SHIPPING ————

SALES TAX ————

TOTAL ————

Add $3.95 postage/handling for the first book ordered and $1.00 for each additional book. Outside North America, please contact us for shipping rates. California residents add 8.5% sales tax. Payment in U.S. dollars only.

* Free book of equal or lesser value. Shipping and applicable sales tax extra.
Cleis Press • (800) 780-2279 • orders@cleispress.com
www.cleispress.com
You'll find more great books on our website.